For the B

"A fun book! It has a little bit of *everything*, from tongue-in-cheek travel tips to romance and recipes (and, oh, are they *good*)."
—**Carole Bugge, author of *Who Killed Blanche DuBois?***

"If you can't afford a Russian cruise up the Volga, this charming murder mystery, which mixes tasty cuisine and a group of frisky, wisecracking, middle-aged chorines, is the next best thing."
—**Charles Salzberg, author of the Shamus Award–**
  nominated *Swann's Last Song*

"The Happy Hoofers bring hilarity and hijinks to the high seas—or in this case, a river cruise across Russia on a ship where murder points to more than a few unusual suspects."
—**Nancy Coco, author of *All Fudged Up***

"A page-turning cozy mystery . . . The cast of characters includes endearing, scary, charming, crazy and irre-sistible people. Besides murder and mayhem, we are treated to women who we might want as our best friends, our shrinks and our travel companions."
—**Jerilyn Dufresne, author of the Sam Darling mystery**
  series

"A huge treat for armchair travelers and mystery fans alike . . . Vivid description and deft touches of local color take the reader right along."
—**Peggy Ehrhart, author of the Maxx Maxwell mystery**
  series

Also by Mary McHugh

Cape Cod Murder
The Perfect Bride
The Woman Thing
Law and the New Woman
Psychology and the New Woman
Careers in Engineering and Engineering Technology
Veterinary Medicine and Animal Care Careers
Young People Talk About Death
*Special Siblings: Growing Up with Someone
with a Disability*
How Not to Become a Little Old Lady
How Not to Become a Crotchety Old Man
How to Ruin Your Children's Lives
How to Ruin Your Marriage
How to Ruin Your Sister's Life
Eat This! 365 Reasons Not to Diet
Clean This! 320 Reasons Not to Clean
Good Granny/Bad Granny
How Not to Act Like a Little Old Lady
*If I Get Hit by a Bus Tomorrow, Here's How
to Replace the Toilet Paper Roll*
Aging With Grace— Whoever She Is
*Go For It: 100 Ways to Feel Young, Vibrant,
Interested and Interesting After 50*

Chorus Lines, Caviar, and Corpses

A Happy Hoofers Mystery

Mary McHugh

KENSINGTON PUBLISHING CORP.
http://www.kensingtonbooks.com

KENSINGTON BOOKS are published by

Kensington Publishing Corp.
119 West 40th Street
New York, NY 10018

All Kensington Titles, Imprints, and Distributed Lines are available at special quantity discounts for bulk purchases for sales promotions, premiums, fund-raising, and educational or institutional use. Special book excerpts or customized printings can also be created to fit specific needs. For details, write or phone the office of the Kensington special sales manager: Kensington Publishing Corp., 119 West 40th Street, New York, NY 10018, attn: Special Sales Department, Phone: 1-800-221-2647.

Kensington and the K logo Reg. U.S. Pat & TM Off.

ISBN-13: 978-1-61773-359-8
ISBN-10: 1-61773-359-8
First Kensington Mass Market Edition: November 2014

eISBN-13: 978-1-61773-360-4
eISBN-10: 1-61773-360-1
First Kensington Electronic Edition: November 2014

10 9 8 7 6 5 4 3 2 1

Printed in the United States of America

To Earl, the light and love of my life

Chapter 1

Keeping On Our Toes

It all started when Mary Louise decided we needed to exercise. We are five close friends, who've all managed to stay fit over the years. Still, when we moved into our fifties, we knew we had to watch what we ate and become more active.

We considered all the ways there are to exercise. What we really loved was dancing, especially tap dancing, so we took a class and worked out some routines. Before long, we were asked to perform at a local senior center . . . and then at a community service luncheon . . . and one gig led to another. Pretty soon the word was out about the fabulous five fifty-somethings with the high kicks, smooth moves, and bright smiles. Our video on YouTube got hundreds of hits.

Who knew we'd get to be so good that someone would hire us to dance on the *Smirnov,* a

Russian ship sailing up the Volga from Moscow to St. Petersburg? That we would encounter a stern German cruise director named Heidi, a disgruntled British chef who loved to drink but wasn't fond of cooking, and a motley crew that never did master the art of graceful service?

We thought we would eat some good food, meet some nice people, see things we'd never seen before, and get paid for it. What could go wrong?

Plenty, as it turned out. If I'd known ahead of time that we'd get mixed up in a couple of murders and that my own life would be endangered on this so-called pleasure trip, I would have stayed happily at home in Champlain, New Jersey, commuting to New York to my job as a travel editor at *Perfect Bride* magazine.

Let me tell you a bit about us.

Just briefly, there's me, Tina Powell, who for better or worse is the leader of our little group because I'm the most organized. Like our whole gang, I'm in good shape because of our dancing. I weigh 110 pounds and am 5′4″ tall. I don't mention that I'm over fifty to strangers because I can read their minds: *Drives a gas-guzzling SUV. Wrapped up in her kids. Belongs to a book club that reads Jane Austen and never gets around to discussing the book. Botox.*" I loved telling my coworkers at *Perfect Bride* magazine, where I'm the travel editor, that my friends and I were hired to dance on a cruise ship in Russia. Their usual reaction was, "You mean they're actually going to pay you?" I would just nod and smile. Besides dancing on this trip, I'm also writing an article for newlyweds who might want to honeymoon on this cruise.

Janice Rogers is an actress and director of shows in community theaters in our town. Since her divorce, she's been busier than ever, especially after her daughter went off to college. She's tall and blond and has an unlined face that never seems to age. Her skin has a glow that makes her look far younger than she is. When we ask her how she keeps her complexion like that, she says, "Neglect. I only wash it once a day. Soap is bad for your skin." She is a fierce friend, always there when you need her. I met her when she moved next door to me just after she and her husband split up.

Janice has long legs and, in black tights, they are stunning. "The legs are the last to go," she says. Actually, we all have great legs—it's just genetic, nothing we did or didn't do. And black stockings hide a multitude of sins.

Pat Keeler, a family therapist, our mother hen, watches over us. She's on the phone whenever she thinks it's necessary to make sure we're all right. She always remembers the tap routines. If we forget, we just look at Pat and do whatever she's doing. She is our rock. Her face is beautiful, with a few worry lines on her forehead. She's usually very serious, but when she smiles, it warms all of us. She's taller than the rest of us.

Oh, and she's gay. It's just a fact of life with her. She doesn't flaunt it or hide it. Many of her clients are gay; she understands what they're going through. The rest of us are straight. Pat helps us with our problems too.

Mary Louise Temple has been my closest friend for over thirty years. We met when we both worked at *Redbook* magazine and became best friends. She has one of those Irish faces, with porcelain skin, dark hair, and blue, blue eyes. She somehow managed to keep a great body after three children and she thinks if you're not Irish, you should at least try. She's the only one who still has a husband, George, who believes it's his job to correct all the mistakes her parents made when they were bringing her up. I never could find any mistakes.

Finally, there's Gini Miller, a fierce redhead with a temper to match. She's a prize-winning documentary filmmaker, small and pretty. She's divorced. "We just wanted different things," she says of her ex-husband. "He was happy sitting on a couch with a beer watching football." She wanted to see the world. She filmed an oral history of the people who lost their homes in Hurricane Katrina in New Orleans. She made a documentary about an orphanage in India, where she fell in love with a little girl she hopes to adopt when regulations ease in that country.

We call ourselves the Happy Hoofers—that's with an *f*.

I love these women. The easy intimacy that

the five of us enjoy has certainly helped to prepare us for life after fifty. We've been through everything together—miscarriages, sick children, husbands' affairs, cancer, widowhood, teenagers, divorce. None of us could have done it without the other four cheering us on, lending a shoulder to cry on, saying just the right words to make everything better.

We are all different, all great-looking, and fierce friends forever.

Tina's Travel Tip: Talk to as many people as you can on a cruise—some of them might actually be interesting.

Chapter 2

Cruising and Schmoozing

I knew this wasn't going to be one of your Love Boat cruises the minute I opened the door to our cabin.

"Mary Louise, look at the size of this room! How can we change into our costumes in here?"

"Wait until you see the bathroom," she said. "There's no bath and I'd hardly call it a room. If we hadn't dieted ourselves into near nonexistence, we wouldn't be able to wash during the whole trip."

I looked over her shoulder and groaned. There was a basin, a toilet, and enough floor space for a very small three-year-old to take a shower.

"Where's the shower?" Mary Louise asked.

"I think you take the faucet off the basin and hang it on that hook up there, pull this curtain around you, and very carefully take a shower without breaking any of your movable parts."

"This is ridiculous," she said. "There's only two feet of floor space between the beds to change our clothes in. We'll have to dress in shifts."

"Too bad—I forgot to pack mine," I said, and we fell on the narrow beds laughing hysterically.

"Remind me again why we decided to take a Russian river cruise," she said.

"Because somebody actually hired us to tap dance on a ship sailing from Moscow to St. Petersburg," I said.

"What were they thinking!" she said.

"What were *we* thinking?" I said, and that set us off again. We couldn't help giggling at the absurdity of this whole situation. We've been friends for such a long time, we can read each other's thoughts. Ever since we met at *Redbook* magazine, where we both worked as editors before we were married, we've been good friends.

We've helped each other through babies—three for her and two for me—marital fights, and musicals at the community theater where she and I danced and sang our way to local stardom and total disdain from our teenagers. And the death of my husband a year ago. I could never have made it without her.

Now, at the age of fifty-two (Mary Louise) and

fifty-three (me), we are on another adventure with our friends Gini, Janice, and Pat.

"Remember that time we drove across the country with Gini and Pat in that old Pontiac?" Mary Louise said. "Some of the places we stayed had smaller bathrooms than this."

"Can you believe we were still friends after four weeks crammed into that ten-year-old car, with a water hose that leaked—"

"And we patched it with bubble gum! You always had to sleep on the rollaway because you were the smallest, Tina. You must have weighed ninety pounds in those days. What do you weigh now?"

"None of your business. Why do you think I took up tap dancing? Let's see if we can unpack our stuff."

"Wait," said Mary Louise, pulling an aerosol can out of her tote bag. "Let me spray the drawers with Lysol first. You never know what might have been in there."

"OK, Ms. Germ Freak," I said. We often tease Mary Louise about her fastidious habits. She's the only person I know who actually sings the entire "Happy Birthday" song while washing her hands.

After unpacking in our crowded little stateroom, somehow finding room to put everything, we collected our friends and headed out to get some breakfast.

* * *

The *Smirnov*'s dining room was a bright and cheerful space, with windows all around. The tables were set with linen tablecloths, blue and white china, crystal glasses, and sparkling silverware. Comfortable yellow wicker chairs complemented red roses, freshly cut and fragrant in a vase in the middle of each table. We sat at a round table for five and waited for a waitress to come and take our order.

Gradually the other tables filled up, but there was still no one to take our order. A little jet-lagged and really hungry, I waved to a large dark-haired woman wearing some kind of naval uniform, who seemed to be in charge.

She strode over to our table and said in a deep voice, "*Ja?*" Her highly polished shoes seemed oversized as they reflected the light.

Hmm, I thought. A German wearing a uniform on a Russian ship? Oh well, just play along.

"Hello," I said. "We were wondering if we could get some breakfast."

"May I see your room keys?" she said, not smiling, looking at us as if we somehow turned up on this ship illegally.

We handed her the little cards that opened our doors and she nodded.

"Ahhh. You are the entertainment," she said. "You dance, *ja?*"

I almost saluted but stopped myself in time.

"Yes, we are the Happy Hoofers and we're really looking forward to this cruise." I hesitated and then timidly asked, "Could I ask who you are?"

She looked annoyed, as if we should certainly know who she was, and said, "I am Heidi Gorsuch, the ship's director of activities. You vill dance tonight after dinner, yes?"

"We're looking forward to it," I said, dredging up my best party hostess smile. "We're so glad to have the chance to perform on your lovely ship. Is there anything else you would like us to do before our performance?"

"Like vat?"

"We could do lap dances for all the men on board," Janice said, and I could see she was just getting warmed up.

I faked a laugh and glared at Janice. "Oh, Ms. Gorsuch, she's just joking. We thought we'd mingle with the other passengers and get to know them. Sort of goodwill tap dancers."

"Is gut," she said, and I could swear she clicked her heels together before moving to the next table.

"Good going, Tina," Gini said. "We're stuck on a Russian ship with a cruise director who talks like a drill instructor, a cabin the size of a broom closet, and no food in sight."

Gini always says exactly what she thinks about everything.

"Relax, Gini," Pat, our peacemaker, said. "We

just got here. Things will get better. Don't make such a big deal about it."

"Listen, happy face, I'm tired and hungry and in no mood to—"

"You want food," a sullen, blond waitress said, appearing from nowhere. Her name tag identified her as Olga.

"Do you have a menu?" Janice asked, smiling as only Janice can.

"No menu," the waitress said, and was about to leave.

"Please," I said. "How do we get something to eat?"

She pointed to a long table on one side of the room that was now covered with food and platters, baskets and samovars.

"You go get what you want," she said. "You want drink?"

"I'd like some orange juice," I said, and my friends ordered the same.

"Could you put a little vodka in mine?" Pat asked.

Olga looked at her as if she had ordered a hit of heroin, then walked off.

We got in line at the buffet table, which was loaded with croissants, muffins and breads, scrambled eggs kept warm in a metal container, jams and butter and bacon, sausage, and waffles. A man stood behind the table ready to whip up any kind of omelet you wanted.

I was behind a woman wearing a pale pink

11

sweater over a rather plain beige dress. Because I have this habit of talking to people wherever I go—it used to drive my husband Bill crazy—I said to her, "Looks really good, doesn't it?"

She didn't turn around, but said with a very pronounced British accent, "I'mnotveddygood-inthemorning."

"Excuse me?" I said, leaning forward to hear her better.

She exhaled a long-suffering sigh, and said more slowly, "I'm not veddy good in the morning. Pahdon me." She picked up her plate of toast and a boiled egg and walked to her table.

I felt boorish, crass, like an ugly American.

"I see you're making friends in your usual effective way," Mary Louise said, laughing.

"Oh, shut up," I said, recovering my dignity and asking the man behind the table for a salmon omelet.

We were just digging into the first food we had eaten in twelve hours when a loud whistle startled us and made us turn. Heidi, lips still pursed from her ear-splitting signal, stood at the front of the room.

"Gut morning," she said, clapping her hands together like the principal in a boarding school and arranging her face in what I'm sure she hoped was a smile.

"Velcome, velcome," she said in a loud voice to the startled passengers. "I am Heidi, your cruise director. Ve haf many fun things planned for you on this cruise and you *vill* enjoy them. Please ask me if you have questions. Our Russian crew will do their best to help you, but they sometimes have trouble with the English. Some of them are just learning their jobs. I'm sure you will be patient with them." From the look in her eye, I was sure she was giving us orders, not asking for our cooperation.

"I vant first to introduce our captain. Captain Kurt Von Schnappel."

A tall, grim-faced man with gray hair in a dark blue naval uniform stepped forward and surveyed the crowd in front of him. I couldn't help feeling that he disapproved of us and that saying hello was a distasteful part of his job.

"*Guten morgen,*" he said. "Enjoy your voyage." He gave a slight bow and left the dining room. That was it. No friendly welcome. No "glad to see you." I assumed we wouldn't be getting an invitation to sit at the captain's table anytime soon.

Heidi watched him go, then motioned to the white-suited crew members. They stepped forward, their hands folded, looking down at the floor.

"Oh dear," Gini said under her breath. "What have we done?"

"Now I vould like to introduce the crew to you. First is Sasha, who is in charge of the dining room."

Sasha stepped forward, his eyes darting wildly

13

from side to side, desperately searching for a way to escape. His uniform jacket was buttoned crookedly, leaving one side longer than the other, and his shirt tail was untucked in the back. His hair stuck out all over his head as if it were trying to escape. Surely no older than twenty-five, he looked as if he couldn't be in charge of a falafel stand on a street corner in New York City, let alone a dining room on a cruise ship.

"Next ve haf our chef, Kenneth Allgood from England, who comes to us highly recommended. He vill prepare many delicious Russian meals for you—but with a British accent—and you vill enjoy them."

"A British chef on a Russian ship," a man in back of us muttered. "What's his specialty— Spotted Chicken Kiev?"

I turned around and saw a handsome man about my age, with dark hair graying at the temples, at a table near us. He looked like a golfer in his seersucker slacks and short-brimmed cap. I smiled at him and he smiled back.

The chef stepped forward unsteadily, a cigarette dangling from his mouth, wearing filthy whites with a toque perched on top of his greasy hair. He looked about twenty-eight years old. He glared at the passengers.

"Geeez," Gini said in a low voice. "His mother must have been Typhoid Mary."

I tried to give her a stern glance, but I was also trying to keep from laughing. If I looked at

Mary Louise, we would both lose it. Out of the corner of my eye, I could see her stifling a giggle.

Heidi introduced the waitresses, the desk clerks, and the kitchen crew, and then she said, "Ve haf a special treat for you on this trip. Ve are very lucky to have with us the Happy Hoofers from America, who vill tap dance for us tonight and every night of the cruise. Please stand up, Hoofers."

We stood up and smiled at the other passengers, who clapped rather halfheartedly. Who could blame them? This cruise was not turning out to be the polished, interesting, professionally run trip they had been hoping for. And, of course, they had never heard of us.

"Happy Hookers?" an old man at the table next to us snarled. "What kind of a cruise is this? I don't want to see a bunch of hookers."

His wife tried to shush him. "They're *hoofers*, dear, not hookers. You know, dancers." But he kept on grumping and snarling until she pulled him out on the deck. As she dragged him away, she said over her shoulder, "He's been this way since Hillary ran for president."

We had another cup of good strong coffee and looked out the window at the clear, sunny day brightening the clean, white deck outside. I was glad we were making this trip in June when the temperature would be in the sixties and seventies.

We walked out to the deck and leaned on the rail as the ship glided by little towns, with brilliantly colored red and blue and green church domes peeking over the treetops, people picnicking along the riverbanks, and fishermen who waved to us holding rods.

"If that's their idea of breakfast, I can't wait to see lunch and dinner. What a crew of misfits. Why do I have the impression I'm on the Russian equivalent of the *Titanic*?" Gini said.

"Let's throw Debbie Downer overboard right now," Janice said, grabbing Gini by the arm.

"Look on the bright side, Gini," Pat said. "How else could we get to see Moscow and St. Petersburg and the Hermitage Museum?"

"We'll be lucky if this crew can get us to the next town without running into another ship," Gini said. "At least we can look forward to seeing the White Nights at this time of year. I'll be able to take pictures twenty-four hours a day if I want."

"Think of this trip as a great setting for a documentary," I said.

"Riiiight. Look on the bright side," Gini said. "You're always such an optimist, Tina. You remind me of that Monty Python movie, *Life of Brian*. Brian is nailed to a cross, and he says, 'Peter, I can see your house from up here!' Then he sings, 'Always Look on the Bright Side of Life.' "

That's all we needed to hear. We linked arms

and sang the rest of the song, dancing and twirling on deck.

Passengers gathered around us, clapping and laughing as we did some time steps and high kicks.

Even Gini was in a good mood after our impromptu practice session.

Two teenaged girls bounced up to us. "Are you the Happy Hoofers?" asked the one with dark hair with pink streaks on the side, who looked about seventeen years old.

"We are," I said. "Do you like tap dancing?"

"Oh yes," she said, "It's cool. We saw a musical on Broadway with Savion Glover. I love that kind of dancing. He has so much energy."

"We want to be your groupies," the younger one, around fourteen with curly blonde hair, said. "We saw you on YouTube, and half our class is taking tap dancing now. We could help you with scenery, or costumes, or anything you need. I'm Andrea and this is Stacy."

"We don't really have scenery and we already have costumes, but you're welcome to watch us rehearse," I said. "We'll teach you some steps. What are you doing on a cruise ship in Russia anyway?"

"Our grandmother brought us. She's celebrating her eightieth birthday and she thought it would be more fun if she took us with her."

"And I was right," an older woman said, coming up to join us. She had a face she had earned after eighty years of a good life—beautiful, lined, serene, ready for anything that came along. "Hello there, Hoofers," she said, and did a little time step and a ball change. "I'm Caroline. These are my two spoiled-rotten granddaughters, who are the joy of my life. Can't wait to see you dance tonight. I do a little tap dancing myself."

"Nana was one of the dancing Kennard sisters in the fifties," Stacy said. "She was really good, and she still is. She used to take us to Macy's Tap-a-thon every year in New York—that's why we love tap dancing."

"You're kidding," I said. "Mary Louise and I went every year for a while."

Her mention of the Tap-a-thons brought back all those hot August mornings when Mary Louise and I would drive into New York and put on some kind of cartoon T shirt—Mickey Mouse, Betty Boop, Garfield, whatever they thought up that year—and join people of all ages, colors, and states of mental health, to dance on Broadway in front of Macy's.

"Hi, Caroline," Mary Louise said. "We had so much fun at those Tap-a-thons. The best part was, after we danced, Tina and I would go to the fanciest restaurant we could find, still in our sweaty T shirts and tap shoes, and eat up all the calories we had just danced off. The last time we went, there were six thousand other people out there in Betty Boop T shirts and lace garters dancing on Thirty-fourth Street."

"We were part of the six thousand," Caroline said. "We were probably right in back of you."

"You would have pretended you didn't know us if you were anywhere nearby," I said. "We kept forgetting the routine and asking the trainer to do it over again. Then we figured if we made a mistake, who would notice? We had a great time. I don't know why they stopped doing them."

"They probably couldn't find anyone crazy enough to organize them after the woman who did them for years retired," Caroline said.

"Nana was always the best," Stacy said. "She helped the ones who were stumbling around. But the whole thing was really fun. I wish they still did it."

"Me too," I said. "Come on, Caroline. Show us what you've got."

Caroline smiled. She sang a verse of "Always Look on the Bright Side of Life" in a still-young soprano, breaking into a time step and grapevine that brought applause from the crowd that had gathered around us.

"How do you stay so young?" Mary Louise asked.

"These two girls are the main reason. And tap dancing is great exercise. My sister and I taught dancing until a few years ago. Then I decided to travel and have a good time. But I miss the dancing."

"Come watch us whenever you want, Caroline," I said. "I'm sure you could teach us a few

19

steps—as well as a lot of other things. Here's my cell – call me any time you want to find us."

"I'll stay out of your way, but if you can put up with these two, they'd love it," she said, reaching out to hug her granddaughters.

"You got it," Mary Louise said. "They're welcome anytime they want to come watch us rehearse. We'll put them to work."

A young man with shoulder-length blond hair tapped Janice on the shoulder. He was about twenty-eight, around 5′10″ tall, a little taller than Janice. His features were handsome, delicate. "Excuse me," he said, "but aren't you Janice Rogers?"

"I am," she said.

"I saw you in a play in Princeton one time. I always wanted to meet you. I'm an actor too. "

"Always glad to meet another actor," Janice said, her face lighting up the way it usually does when she gets to talk about the theater. "What play did you see?"

" '*Who's Afraid of Virginia Woolf?*' You were brilliant."

"That's a great play," Janice said. "I was lucky to get that part. What's your name?"

"Brad Sheldon."

"Are you working?"

"Sort of. I'm going to be in an off-Broadway production in the fall. A new play."

"What's your role?"

"I'm a schizophrenic medical student."

"You are not!" Janice said, laughing.

"I'm not kidding. Any help you can give me will be gratefully accepted."

"I'd like to try," Janice said, moving closer to the young actor. "This is a real challenge. I always think the gestures you make are an important part of defining your character."

"What kind of gestures do you think my schizophrenic would make?" Brad asked.

"I think he would use his hands a lot. He sort of talks with his hands. He'd get into the part physically—when he's excited, he'd move his whole body a lot and use his hands to make a point. Like this," said Janice, gesturing and reaching out to touch Brad while she talked. "See what I mean?"

"You're right," Brad said. "I've been so busy concentrating on saying the lines that I didn't think about my gestures. What else?"

"It's all about pretending you are schizophrenic. You should read up on that illness and figure out how it presents itself physically. Did you pretend to be different people when you were a kid?"

"Oh sure," Brad said. "Lots of times."

"That's all acting is . . . What did you say your name is . . . Brad?" Janice said. "The best actors I know just pretend they're someone else and have fun doing it."

"Is that what you do?" he asked.

"Of course. It's easy when you look at any part that way."

"This is really helpful," Brad said. "What else should I—"

The British chef, still in his stained whites, stepped in front of Janice. "Sorry to interrupt your acting lessons," he said to Brad. "I noticed you before when Heidi was introducing us. I'm Ken Allgood. Are you an American?"

"Yes, from New York," Brad said.

"Great city, that. I was there a couple of years ago and I'm going back as soon as I can. Maybe open my own restaurant. Best food ever there."

"Where did you go?" Brad asked, with an apologetic shrug to Janice.

We moved to the rail to admire the scenery, but we couldn't help overhearing the two men's conversation.

"All over. There was this one place—downtown somewhere. Right inside the door when you walked in there were all these apples—the smell was incredible. The dining room had dark red walls and an arched ceiling. And the food! Every mouthful was perfect."

"That sounds like Brigantine. I know someone who works there," Brad said. "I'll introduce you if you do get back to New York. Maybe he can get you a job."

"I say! You mean it? That would be great. We

have to talk. What are you doing on this bonkers cruise ship anyway?"

"Well, I—I was supposed to come with my friend Maxim," Brad said, hesitating. He looked around the deck at the other passengers gathered in small groups, breathing in the clear, fresh air and talking to each other. "He's from Russia. He was going to introduce me to his parents. And he wanted to show me St. Petersburg. He said it was the most beautiful city in the world. He wanted to take me to the Hermitage and to Catherine Palace, and everywhere. We bought our tickets six months ago and then–" Brad stopped and turned away. There were tears in his eyes.

The chef touched his arm. "What happened?"

"He met somebody else. We lived together for a year and then he just left. At first, I wasn't going to go on this cruise, but I really wanted to see Russia because I had heard so much about it from him. But it's not the same. This trip would have been so great with him along. Now it just reminds me of him."

He stared at the river stretching ahead of us. My heart went out to this fragile young man who was obviously in so much pain. I was about to invite him to join us for some coffee later, but before I could say anything, Allgood put his arm around Brad's shoulder.

"Maybe I can help," he said. "Come on. I'll

buy you a coffee and help you forget. We'll talk about New York. I still have some time before I have to get back to the kitchen."

Brad hesitated, then took a deep breath and smiled at the chef. "You're on."

"There's something about that Ken guy I don't like," Janice said to me. "I don't know why exactly, but I don't trust him."

"I know what you mean," I said. "He's got this sneaky way about him. Let's hope he can cook."

"Good luck on that one," the man who had been sitting in back of us at breakfast said. Up close, he was tall, and even better looking than I'd noticed in the dining room. He had one of those craggy faces—like Harrison Ford when he made the Indiana Jones movies about raiding lost arks. His hair was mostly brown with a little gray at the temples, and he was wearing the rimless glasses I love on a man. Bill used to wear them and so did my father. To me, they meant a man who is really smart, really in charge, really sexy. My kind of man.

"Hi," he said to me. "I'm Barry Martin. How did you get to tap dance in the middle of the Volga River?"

"Hello," I said. "I'm Tina Powell. My friends and I made a short video of our act and put it on YouTube. The agent for this cruise line saw it and hired us. We decided we were up for an adventure. What are you doing here?"

"It seemed like a good idea at the time," he

said, smiling. He was even better-looking when he smiled. "I've been everywhere else but I've never been to Russia. Now I'm not so sure it was a good idea."

"You can't judge by the first couple of hours. Give it a chance. Maybe the food will be better than you think."

He looked at me and hesitated. I could see that he wanted to ask me something but wasn't sure if he should. I waited. I was feeling really good about myself that morning. I had on a light blue top that made my eyes look bluer, and my hair curved around both sides of my face the way it's supposed to when I use the dryer just right. I'd had it highlighted before we went on the cruise, so it was exactly the color I wish I had been born with. I could tell he liked the way I looked.

"Did your husband come with you?" he asked.

"My husband died last year," I said.

I swallowed hard. It's still hard to talk about Bill. I can't believe he's really gone. We married young—I was twenty-three and he was twenty-five. We both read everything that wasn't locked up, traveled whenever we had enough money, loved foreign films, saved every Friday night for a date, just the two of us, and never ran out of things to tell each other. I fell asleep in his arms every night for nearly 30 years.

"I'm sorry," Barry said. "You must miss him a lot."

"Every day," I said, the words catching in my throat. "He was my best friend."

"Did you say your name was Powell?" he asked. I nodded, and he said, "You know, there was a guy named Bill Powell in my class at law school. I don't suppose it's the same guy."

"Bill graduated from Yale Law School in 1982."

"It is the same guy. I knew him—not well, but I knew him."

I did a double take. "You're kidding. You really were in the same class with Bill? I don't believe it. Oh, we have to talk."

"How about right now?" Barry said, taking my hand. "Let's get some coffee."

"I can't, Barry," I said, torn between pleasure and duty. "I have to gather my troops and rehearse for our dance tonight. But I'd love to talk after our performance."

"Looking forward to it. See you then."

He leaned over and gently smoothed my hair back. Something I hadn't felt in a long time, that feeling that I wanted a man to kiss me, enveloped me, but I stepped back and said, "See you then."

Tina's Travel Tip: If you're going on a Russian cruise ship, make sure the chef is Russian. A British chef probably isn't a good idea.

Chapter 3

Make 'em Laugh

I signaled to my pals, who moved to surround me.

"Who was that guy you were talking to, Tina?" Mary Louise asked. "He's gorgeous."

"He is, isn't he?" I said. "His name is Barry. He was in Bill's class at law school. What are the chances of that?"

"Work it, honey," she said. "It's time you got back in action."

"No action. Just a drink after our performance tonight."

"You know what they say," Mary Louise said. "Some things you never forget how to do."

"Bite your tongue. I'm not ready for that either."

"It's not really a question of being ready," Mary Louise said teasingly. "It just happens. You know, it's like riding a bicycle. You never forget how."

"That reminds me of something Gloria Steinem said," I said, thinking aloud.

"What?"

"A woman without a man is like a fish without a bicycle," I said.

"One of these days you're going to want another bicycle," she said, laughing.

"I think we should rehearse our dance for tonight," I said, changing the subject. "We're doing 'Singin' in the Rain' and we need to figure out how we're going to do this in the Skylight Bar. Most people are on deck or unpacking, so let's go in there now."

"Good idea," our official worrier, Pat, said, "We've never danced there before."

There was nobody in the bar except the teenagers, Stacy and Andrea, who were sipping lattes and giggling.

"Will we bother you girls if we do a little rehearsing in here?" I asked.

"Are you kidding?" Stacy said. "We'd love it! Can we watch?"

"Sure."

We turned on the CD player and swung into our flaps, shuffles, hops, cramp rolls, ball changes, buffaloes, grapevines, time steps, riffs, and shim shams. Stacy and Andrea could not sit still. They got in back of us and tried to copy our steps. They improvised their own moves and then did an impromptu performance for us when we finished. At the end, we were all panting to catch our breaths.

"Not bad," Mary Louise said. "You can fill in if one of us breaks a leg."

"We don't want you to break anything," Andrea said, her blue eyes twinkling.

"No," Stacy said, tossing her head. "Maybe just a sprained ankle or something."

"Thanks a lot," I said. "That's all we need."

My phone vibrated. "Hi, Caroline," I said. "Are you looking for your granddaughters? We've decided to keep them. Do you need them? I'll tell them."

"Your Nana is looking for you girls," I said. "She wants you to come and help her find something."

"We'll be back," Stacy said. "Don't go away."

We were about to swing into our routine again when we heard the sound of tapping coming from the other end of the room. Janice's new friend Brad danced across the floor like a spinning top, leaping and jumping and cartwheeling to the music, making Donald O'Connor faces as his blond hair flew. His dancing was funny, graceful, effortless.

29

"Hey," Janice said, "you're good. I didn't know you could dance too."

"I try to learn everything—dancing, singing, acting, mime—so I can keep working," Brad said. "I can't really dance—I just pretend. And that coffee I had with Ken was so strong, I feel like I could dance over the moon." He flopped down on a chair. "But not right now."

"Want to do a couple of cartwheels and spins in our act when we change costumes in the middle?" I said. "You'd be great."

"I can't," he said. "I'd love to, but I promised Ken I'd meet him tonight after dinner."

"How come you're not with him now?" Janice asked.

"He had to go browbeat the kitchen staff. He says they're terrible. None of them speaks English and they don't know how to make the things he wants to serve. The whole thing is a mess. I feel sorry for him. I'm going to meet him after lunch and we're going to talk about starting a restaurant together in New York."

"You make it sound easy," Janice said. "Where are you going to get the money for all this?"

"Ken said we'll figure it out. He says if I can just help him get to New York, we'll do it."

"Why does he need you to help him? Can't he just go on his own?" Janice was clearly skeptical of the chef's fantasies.

"Well," Brad said, and hesitated, "I don't know what happened exactly, but he was in some kind of trouble and is having a problem getting a visa. He said if I sponsor him, he could get into the United States at least temporarily and then figure out how to stay permanently."

This didn't sound right at all. I didn't want to say anything because what did I know about visas and getting into the United States?

Gini, of course, had no trouble wading right in.

"What are you—crazy?" she said. "You better find out what kind of trouble he was in before you start sponsoring him. You don't know what he did."

"That's all in the past," Brad said. "The thing is, I really like him."

"Why?" Gini said. "He doesn't seem all that great to me."

Brad crossed his arms, seeming to hug himself. "It's the way he looks at me." He looked embarrassed, then continued. "I can tell he really cares about me. He makes me feel good about myself. He really listens to me, lets me pour my heart out to him about Maxim. I need that right now."

"You just met him," Gini said. She tried to speak calmly, but for Gini that's hard. "You don't know anything about him."

"She's right, Brad," Janice said. "Don't get too involved with him. He doesn't look very reliable to me. I'm only telling you this because I don't want to see you get hurt. Are you sure he's not just using you to get to New York?"

Brad pushed back his chair and stood up. "You don't know anything about him either," he said angrily. "I like him and I want to know him better."

"Just be careful," Janice said.

He looked at her and started to say something, but then turned abruptly and walked out of the bar.

"I hope he knows what he's doing," Janice said, her face reflecting the worry she felt for this boy. "I hope that he doesn't rush into anything. He's so vulnerable right now."

"Stay out of it, Jan," Gini said. "It's none of our business."

Nobody said anything. We all felt uncomfortable. Then Mary Louise, our peacemaker, who hates it when we fight, said, "Are we going to rehearse or what?"

I looked around at these good friends and smiled. "Let's do it," I said. "Too bad Brad won't be here to do a little clowning, but we'll have to do without him."

"You need clowns?" Stacy said, coming back into the room with her sister. "We can do that. Watch."

She and Andrea proceeded to do a perfect clown act complete with tumbles, cartwheels, and even did a split.

"You're hired," I said. "See if you can come up with some kind of clown outfit by tonight. You can be part of our act."

"Wait til Nana hears we're in show biz," Andrea said, running off with Stacy, both of them giggling.

"They're so young," Pat said with a sigh. "I've almost forgotten what it's like to be a teenager. They've got their whole lives ahead of them. Hope they make the right choices."

"Did you make the right choices when you were their age?" Janice asked. "I was already pregnant by then. And I'd probably make the same mistake again today. You're just not wise and careful and sensible when you're that young."

"I was," Pat said sadly. "I was too sensible, too afraid to take chances, too cautious. But I see what happens every day in my practice when you don't follow the rules, when you just do whatever you feel like. You hurt yourself and you hurt others."

"I'd rather take chances and make mistakes and put up with the pain," Janice said. "I'd rather die than just sit huddled in a corner worrying that I might do something wrong, playing it safe . . ." She paused, looked at Pat, and added, "Drinking too much."

"I don't drink any more than the rest of you," Pat said defensively. "Anyway, it relaxes me."

"I'm not the one who had vodka in my orange juice at breakfast," Janice said. "But hey, who cares? It's your liver."

"At least I didn't end up like you, with three

failed marriages and a daughter who doesn't speak to you," Pat said. It was unlike her to react so sharply, but it was obvious she resented Janice's remark about her drinking. We had all noticed that Pat seemed to be drinking more lately than she usually did, but this was the first time any of us had brought it up.

Janice looked as if she'd been slapped. "Leave my Sandy out of this, Pat. She's been drug- free for three years now and is doing well. I've always loved her and tried to shield her from my own problems. One of these days, she'll understand that I did my best and we'll be friends again. But right now, it hurts to talk about her." There were tears in her eyes.

Pat put her arm around her friend. "Oh, Janice, I'm sorry. I didn't mean to say that. I was just hitting back at you for making me realize how cautious I've always been, how dull my life has been most of the time."

Janice hugged her back. "You've helped a lot of people, Pat," she said. "I wish I'd known you when I was eighteen."

"Me too," Pat said. "I would have had a lot more fun."

"Let's go get some lunch," Mary Louise said, obviously relieved that her two friends had made up. Mary Louise hates any kind of anger or unpleasantness. She wants everything to be nice-nice-nice all the time. I guess that's the way she's dealt with George, who is angry a lot. She just smiles and waits out the storm. I would have left him years ago.

We found a table in the large, bright dining room. Through the windows on three sides we could see the boats sailing by—some pleasure yachts, some working vessels, all churning the water to white foam behind them. Around us the tables filled up with the other passengers. Most were Americans, with some Russians and Brits sprinkled in. The atmosphere seemed livelier than when we ate breakfast in there a few hours before. We heard more laughter and spirited conversations.

The young Russian waitresses lined up along the side until everyone was seated before approaching us to take orders. They looked nervous.

Our server Olga appeared unsmiling at our table. "What do you want?" she asked.

"How is the Petrosavodsky Sudak?" Gini asked.

She shrugged. "Maybe good," she said.

"What is it?" I asked.

The waitress pointed to the menu, which described the dish as "pike perch in potatoes crust with Mediterranean vegetables."

"Potatoes crust sounds terrible—sort of like what's left in the pan after you cook the potatoes. But I'll try it," Gini said.

We all ordered the perch, and looked around

at the other passengers while we waited for our meal. There was an American family at a table nearby, a mother and father and their two well-behaved small children, who had obviously traveled a lot with their parents. At another table, four women traveling together all talked at the same time, laughing and interrupting each other like old friends. A young couple, obviously newlyweds, were holding hands across a table. I remembered my honeymoon in Hawaii. Bill and I couldn't stop talking to each other. We were so glad to be married and together all the time.

When our lunch arrived, Gini took one bite, put down her knife and fork, and said, "This is inedible. The vegetables taste like my mother sneaked into the kitchen and boiled the life out of them. I think I'll try our other choice—braised lamb leg with green beans and potato gratin on thymus. Is that a gland or do they mean thyme?"

Heidi stomped over to our table. She must have noticed our dissatisfied expressions.

"You are enjoying your lunch, no?" she said.

"Right, Heidi," Gini said. "We are enjoying our lunch, no. This food is really bad. I was hoping for some delicious Russian meals on this trip. You know—some stroganoff or chicken Kiev or blinis. How come you hired a British chef? Couldn't you find a Russian one?"

"Mr. Allgood is very good at preparing Russian food so that the Americans and the British passengers will like it." She delivered her line with stern seriousness, as though she had memorized it.

"Well, not this American passenger," Gini said. "This is really bad."

Heidi looked distraught. Her voice dropped an octave. "Vould you like the lamb instead?" she said "The British are very good with mutton."

"It's worth a try, Heidi," I said. "This is not good."

Heidi strode off to the kitchen. We heard loud voices shouting at each other and pots and pans banging on counters. The kitchen door slammed open. Chef Allgood stormed over to our table and glared at us.

"Are you the ones complaining about the lunch?" he demanded. His words were slightly slurred, and a strong smell of beer wafted around him. "I should have known. Americans wouldn't know good food if they fell in it. Anyway, you should try cooking anything on this crazy ship. Nobody understands English. In spite of what you think, I'm a good cook. You're not helping by sending Heidi into the kitchen to yell at me. I'm doing the best I can."

"Well, your idea of Russian cooking is really bad," Gini said. "It's not even good British cooking."

"I could make great food in that kitchen if they'd give me some decent people to work with," Allgood said, "or at least one person who can speak English and understand what I'm trying to tell him. A bunch of food snobs, you and your friends are." He pulled himself up straighter. "I studied at the Manchester Culinary School. It is the best."

"Maybe you should open a restaurant in Manchester," Gini said.

"What do you know? You're American. All you Yanks eat are hot dogs and cheeseburgers."

"We know good cooking from bad," Gini said. "Whatever gave you the idea you could cook Russian food?"

"That's what they hired me to do," he said. "They told me 'Americans and Brits don't want real Russian food. They want Russian food that tastes like the junk they eat in restaurants at home.'"

"Well, whoever *they* are—they're wrong," Gini said. "Some of the finest restaurants in the world are in New York, and we know good food from bad. We're not the only ones who are complaining, anyway. Look at the faces on the other passengers." She pointed to a table near the window where two couples were poking at their food, frowning, and grousing about it to each other in Russian.

"I'm warning you," he said, pointing his finger at Gini—always a mistake, "if you send anybody else into my kitchen like you just did, you're gonna find something rotten in your chicken Kiev."

"Are you threatening me?" Gini said, throwing her napkin on the table and standing up to confront him. The fact that he towered over her didn't faze her in the least.

He leaned closer to her. "I'm just telling you I'm not putting up with any more of your criticisms."

A uniformed arm grabbed him. Heidi's angry face, nose to nose with the chef, glared at him. "Mr. Allgood, you are needed in the kitchen— NOW. I suggest you march yourself in there immediately and prepare some lamb for these ladies."

Allgood glared back. "You try to get those dumb Russians to do what I tell them to do," he said. "No one could turn those idiots into cooks."

He turned and tripped over a chair nearby. The other passengers looked away as he stumbled past their tables on his way to the kitchen.

"I am very sorry," Heidi said to Gini. "He has been drinking. I cannot put up with him until the end of the cruise. One way or another, I'll have to get rid of him." Her voice seemed to get deeper with every sentence.

"How did he get this job, anyway?" Gini asked, calming down.

"Someone in the cruise line's home office in London hired him," Heidi said. "I think he is somebody's brother-in-law. Obviously they didn't investigate him very thoroughly. Now I'm stuck without a decent chef on this cruise. My problem is I don't know vare to find another chef in the middle of the Volga River. If I were back home in Stuttgart, I would have my pick of great cooks." She seemed on the verge of tears.

"The cruise line should send you a replacement, Heidi," Gini said. "They're losing customers this way. Who wants to go on a cruise and come back hungry? Food is the main topic of conversation on a cruise and it shouldn't be 'Ugh' or 'Yuk' or 'What is this stuff?' "

"I know, I know," Heidi said. "You vant the lamb? I get it for you."

"Don't bother, Heidi," I said, trying to reassure her. "I'm not really hungry anyway. We'll get something to eat later."

"No later," Heidi said. "Ve eat at mealtime. That's it. This is not a Carnival Cruise."

"We'll be fine, Heidi," I said, determined not to laugh.

I looked around the table at my four best friends. Their usual cheerful faces were glum. I felt guilty. I was the one who persuaded them to come on this crazy cruise, which was turning out to be a horror story.

"I'm sorry, gang," I said. "Fine mess I've gotten us into. Forgive me?"

"It's not your fault, Tina," Pat said, reaching over to squeeze my hand. "How could you know it would be like this? It's only for a week. And we'll probably lose a couple of pounds. Won't be all bad."

Everybody but Gini laughed. "It'll be bad enough," she said.

"It's OK, honey," Mary Louise said. "We forgive you. And I have some Oreos in my suitcase. You can have one."

"Gee, can you spare it?" I said. "What I really want is to move my body. I feel sluggish. Think I'll change and take a couple of laps around the deck. Anybody else want to come?"

"It'll just make me hungrier," Janice said. "I'm going somewhere quiet and read."

My other three pals waved good-bye. "Have fun, Tina."

I moved into an easy run, breathing in the clear crisp air, the stillness. We were gliding through a tree-lined section of the river as the sun sent slanting rays through the leaves. My brisk pace quieted all the nagging thoughts about where my life was going without Bill, about our performance coming up tonight, about being alone. I started around the deck for my second lap, increasing my speed, the endorphins kicking in to give me a euphoric joy in this day, this adventure, this feeling that right now everything was perfect.

As I rounded the corner on the deck, I saw a figure who hadn't been there before. Chef Kenneth Allgood was leaning on the rail, smoking and watching me as I approached. As I passed by him, he reached out and grabbed my arm.

"I want to talk to you, Yank," he said.

I tried to pull away, but he pushed me against the rail and put an arm on either side of me, pinning me in. He leaned close, his breath stinking of beer, his face bristly with the stubble of his beard.

"Get out of my way," I said.

"What's the matter, don't you like younger men?" he said, grinning at me.

"I just don't like you," I said, struggling to get away from him. "Move."

I tried to push him away, but he pressed his body against me and brought his face closer to mine.

"If you and your friends say anything else bad about my cooking, you're not going to be doing much more running. I could lose my job because of you whining to Heidi like that. So shut up."

I tried to wrench free, but he was too strong for me. He tightened his grip on my arms and brought his face even closer to mine.

I was about to bring my knee up hard between his legs when two strong arms grabbed him and knocked him to the deck.

"If you ever touch her again, I'll break both your arms," Barry said.

The chef glared at him.

"I mean it," Barry said, leaning over him. All-good rolled away from him and stood up, rubbing his arm and limping toward the door, looking back at Barry and me as if he could kill us.

"Are you OK, Tina?" Barry said.

"Oh, Barry. I'm so glad to see you. Could you walk me back to my cabin? I can't stop shaking."

He put his arm around me and supported me down the stairs and through the corridor. I was grateful for his strength because I was really having trouble walking.

When we got to my room, I leaned against the door.

"Are you sure you're all right?" Barry asked. "You don't look all right."

"I'll be OK as soon as I have a shower," I said. "I feel dirty all over."

"I'll be back to check on you later," Barry said. "I'm going to tell Heidi to fire Allgood."

I looked at my rescuer and gave him a weak smile. "Thanks again, Barry."

When I opened the door, Mary Louise took one look at me and grabbed me to help me sit on the bed. "What happened to you? Tina, you look terrible! What's the matter?"

I told her about my unpleasant encounter with Chef Allgood, my voice shaking.

"He can't get away with that," Mary Louise said. "We have to tell Heidi."

"Barry's telling her now," I said, struggling to get to my feet and then sitting down again. "I need a shower."

"Just sit still for a few minutes," Mary Louise said. "Relax, hon, if you can."

When I regained my composure, I stepped into the shower, fumbling with the faucet to hang it on the hook on the wall, wrapping the shower curtain around the drainage hole in the floor and turning on the water.

Cold water dribbled out of the faucet and left me shivering. I kept adjusting the taps. Occasionally, a spurt of hot water made me yelp. I did my best to get clean in this excuse for a shower, and then reached for a towel on the shelf above the toilet. My hand touched only a wire rack. I floundered around trying to find something to dry myself with, but there was nothing.

"Mary Louise," I yelled. "We have no towels. Can you run and get some from the desk person or anyone who looks like they might know where the towels are? Please?"

"Be right back, Tina." I heard her close the door as she left.

Ten minutes later, she still hadn't come back. I was wet and cold and mad.

When the door finally opened, I said, "Where have you been?"

"Here, take this, Tina," she said, handing me a cloth the size of a dish rag. "I'm sorry, but when I told the Russian girl at the desk what I wanted, she said, 'Oh, did you want towels in your room?' I didn't kill her. I said, 'Yes, I have a very wet, very cold, very angry person in my cabin who will strangle you if you don't produce two towels this minute.' It took her forever to round up these miserable things. She probably took them from some other cabin."

"Thanks, Mary Louise. I didn't mean to yell. We'll get Heidi to do something about this. I think in the cruise industry, no hot water and no towels is punishable by death."

"I'd like to think so."

I dried myself as best I could with the thin little scrap of terrycloth Mary Louise had given me. I had the uneasy feeling that this cruise was not going to be the carefree, fun-filled trip we had thought it would be.

Tina's Travel Tip: You should probably ask what's in a drink before you order it on a Russian cruise.

Chapter 4

Can I Buy You A Drink?

That night after dinner, every seat in the Skylight Bar was filled, and people were standing along the sides. They started to clap as soon as Heidi announced, "The Happy Hoofers are here to entertain you tonight. Please give them a warm welcome."

The audience cheered us as we danced out from behind the bar in our very short, pink, filmy baby-doll nighties, with sheer sleeves and V necks. We wore flesh-toned tights and pink tap shoes.

"Good mornin'," we sang in our best Debbie Reynolds voices and danced out onto the floor, arms linked, high-kicking, dipping, lunging, grapevining, time stepping, flapping, shuffling off to Buffalo, to say nothing of ball changes, and just having a blast. Ending with our arms held out to the audience, low bows and a thank you, we tapped backward behind our screen to put on our clown wigs, while Stacy and Andrea bounded out in their polka-dot pajamas and clown makeup. Their high-powered, teen-aged energy could have provided enough electricity to light up the whole ship.

Cart-wheeling, bumping into each other, somersaulting, blowing kisses to the audience, making silly faces—they were a huge hit. The entire audience rose to its feet and cheered them on. One last blare of their noisemakers and they tumbled out of the room as we tapped in and continued the clown act, dipping and circling and step-hopping, flap doodling, and scuff heeling, all while wearing outrageous bright-colored wigs.

The crotchety old man in the front row, who we'd seen earlier, had turned into one of our biggest fans. He kept yelling, "Go, hookers, go," while his wife kept hissing, "Hoofers! *Hoofers!*"

We ran back behind the screen again as Stacy and Andrea reappeared. They tumbled down the aisle and onto the dance floor, rolling around and turning their backs on the audience. As a finale, they looked up and pretended it had started to rain, covering their heads and running for cover.

47

Out we came, in thigh-topping, bright yellow rain slickers over our flesh-colored tights and pink tap shoes, tapping to Gene Kelly's voice rendition of "Singin' in the Rain." We opened our yellow parasols and twirled them as we danced in the imaginary downpour, stepping off the edge of the dance floor and back up again as if we were stepping on and off the curb the way Gene does in the movie. We swung around the light poles, time-stepped, Irish-hopped, and shuffled our way to a big finish while Stacy and Andreaa showered us with silver confetti.

The audience went wild. Caroline was clapping so hard she had to sit down. After we took our bows and blew kisses to the audience, we ran into the crowd to hug her and tell her how terrific her granddaughters were.

"You've started them on a life of drugs and delinquency," she said to us, laughing.

"They're wonderful, Caroline. You must be so proud of them," I said.

"I am," she said. "Until tonight, of course, they were planning to become lawyers and go into politics and run for the Senate. Now they tell me they're going to tap dance on Broadway. You have a lot to answer for, Hoofers."

"Somehow, I know those girls will be just fine," Mary Louise said. "I doubt very much if they'll be dancers. Whatever they do, they'll have a great time doing it."

"That's what it's all about," Caroline said. "I've tried to teach them that."

"Come on out on deck with us," Gini said. "It's still bright as day out there. These White Nights are incredible, aren't they?"

"Think I'll turn in, Hoofers. I'm slowing down a bit these days."

"Not so anyone can tell," I said. We gave her a good-night hug and watched her wind her way out of the Skylight Bar, stopping to talk to people all along the way.

After changing into a blue silk top and white jeans, I headed back to the deck with Janice. As we passed the small barroom next to the Skylight Bar, Janice grabbed my arm and pointed at the two men seated there talking intently, not noticing anything else going on. I knew right away it was Brad and Ken, and I saw the worried look on Janice's face.

"Don't worry, Jan. Brad will be all right."

She sighed. "Oh, I hope so," she said. "He's a nice kid."

Out on deck, we stretched and breathed in the clear night air. The sky was as bright as noon. It was so different from home. I felt like I had never breathed really clean air before.

"Where did you learn to dance like that?" asked an attractive woman with short blond hair in a white sweater and pants. I hadn't noticed her standing next to me at the railing.

"My mother loved tap dancing. She took me for lessons when I was little," I said. "I'll always be grateful to her because, as I got older, I realized what great exercise it is. We've had so much fun since we started this troupe."

"I could tell that from watching you," she said. "Hi. My name is Sue. My husband thinks you're great."

A tall, distinguished-looking balding man standing next to Sue said, "I'm Mark. You're really good. Great legs too, if you don't mind my saying so."

"I never mind hearing that," I said. "Thanks. Where are you two from?"

"Colorado," Sue said. "I'm a painter and my husband is a publisher. We're celebrating our fortieth anniversary and we wanted something really different. We certainly found it. I wasn't sure how it would turn out, but now I'm glad we came."

"Congratulations," I said. "Are you happy with everything?"

"The food could stand a little improvement," Mark said. "That chef is so bad you'd think he was British."

"He is," I said, laughing. "Heidi said they hired him to cook American versions of Russian food. Not a good idea. Weren't you in the dining room this morning when Heidi introduced him?"

"No, we came in later and saw him for the first time when he yelled at you," Mark said.

"We complained about the food and he almost killed us," I said, deciding not to mention my meeting with him on deck.

"We thought maybe the food was so bad because it was his first meal on the cruise," Sue said. "Let's hope it gets better."

"It couldn't get any worse," said a sandy-haired, good-looking, late-fortyish man joining us. "Someone should do something about that chef so we can have some real Russian cooking, which is excellent."

"How do you know so much about Russian cooking?" I asked.

"I live here," he said. "I've had some of the best meals of my life in Russia. And wait until you get to St. Petersburg—it's like eating in Paris."

"What do you do here?" I asked, surprised by his American accent.

"I work for *The New York Times*," he said. "Head of the news bureau here. My name is Alex Boyer. I really like your dancing. Not exactly the Bolshoi, but the best tapping I've seen in a long time."

"Hi, Alex," I said. "I'm Tina Powell. I'll tell the others that you liked our act. Maybe you could use your influence to get a new chef for the rest of the trip. We'd all be grateful."

"I'll see what I can do," Alex said.

He looked at Gini. "Taking pictures to show the folks at home?" he asked her.

Gini shot him a withering glance. "Yeah. I'm having a slide show for all the neighbors as soon as we get back." She moved farther down the rail and focused on the cloud formation.

"Gini's a documentary film-maker," I said softly. "She's won awards for her films."

"Really? What's her name?"

"Gini Miller."

"No kidding! We did a story on her when she won an award for her coverage of Hurricane Katrina in Louisiana. It was a brilliant film."

"If you don't mind my asking, Alex," I said, "what are you doing on this cruise? I would think you'd seen all of this many times."

"I have—but I'm working on a feature story about tourism in Russia, and I wanted to interview some people taking this cruise for my article."

"If you're interested in my opinion," I said, "I think they have a long way to go."

"Especially in the food department," Alex said. "Real Russian food is so much better than this, Tina. Delicate, light. Their produce, eggs, bread, everything is better, fresher, than in lots of restaurants in the States. Don't judge their food by the Russian restaurants in New York or by the chef on this cruise."

He turned to watch Gini again. When she lowered her camera, he said, "Ms. Miller, I'm sorry.

I didn't realize you were the person who made that extraordinary documentary on Hurricane Katrina." He held out his hand. "I'm Alex. Alex Boyer. How did you find the people you talked to in that film? How did you get them to talk about their lives the way you did?" His words came out in a rush. I could tell that Gini was impressed. She took his hand and the expression on her face changed from wary to friendly.

"Many of them are just natural-born storytellers," she said. "I wanted to do a series of oral histories on people who had lost their homes and had nowhere to go and no money to start all over again. They were black and white, old and young, hopeful and despairing. I just turned my camera on and they started talking and didn't stop until I had to leave."

"Your film is so vivid," Alex said. You could tell he was reliving the documentary. "I'll never forget that woman who lived on her roof in the punishing rain and somehow pulled a rowboat up to put over her head like a little shelter. I'd really like to see more of your work. Are you doing a film about this trip?"

Gini shook her head. "No," she said. "But I keep my camera with me all the time because I never know what will turn up next. It's so different here. Such colors and shapes. Oh look, what's that?" She pointed to the reflection of a lone belfry in the clear water near the shore.

"It was once part of a church built in the seventeenth century that was washed away in a flood, leaving the tower standing alone," Alex said. "We're just passing the town of Uglich." He pronounced it *Oog-litch*.

We could see the onion domes of churches and cathedrals gleaming against the cloudless sky above the trees. They were red and blue and gold.

"Look at those blue domes on that red church," Gini said. "What is that?"

Alex was obviously enjoying his role as guide to such an enthusiastic traveler, who seemed genuinely excited by the beauty and strangeness of the skyline.

"It's called the Church of Dmitri on the Blood. The young son of Ivan the Terrible, whose name was Dmitri, moved to Uglich with his mother in 1584 and was murdered seven years later, probably by order of Boris Gudunov. His body was supposedly found on the spot where they built that cathedral."

Gini leaned toward him. "How come you know so much about this town? You don't sound like your average tourist. What do you do?"

"I work for *The New York Times* in Moscow."

"My favorite paper. Do you like living in Russia?"

"I love it. I never know what's going to happen when I wake up in the morning. I've lived in Paris and Hong Kong and Buenos Aires, but this place is the most fascinating by far."

I could tell by the way they looked at each other that something interesting was going on here.

"Does your wife like Moscow?" Gini said, getting straight to the point in true Gini fashion.

"I'm divorced. My wife loved redecorating our house every year and never wanted to travel farther than the mall. I want to see the whole world before I'm through." Alex paused. "What about you? Are you married?"

Gini looked at him, not sure if she was ready to share personal information with this stranger, then said, "I was. My husband thought my job was to make sure the house was spotless every day. He would have loved your wife."

"Maybe we should introduce them," Alex said, and they laughed.

"It was just that I kept thinking of all the things you could do if you weren't cleaning," Gini said.

"Like what?" Alex asked. "Tell me. What would you do?"

Gini looked out at the water, the clear sky, the villages on shore. "I'd learn to paint, go for a bike ride in the springtime, meet a friend for lunch, make love in the ocean, fly a kite on the beach on Cape Cod," she said, all in one big rush of words. "I used to spray Lemon Pledge in the air and run out the door to roller-skate. I wanted to move to Japan, where there's no furniture to clean, no rugs to vacuum, no beds to make, and only a few rice bowls to wash. My husband worked and watched football. Period. I wanted to see the monasteries in Tibet."

Alex looked at her as if he had found his soul mate. "That's on my list too," he said. "You're an adventure junkie like me."

Gini smiled, showing the dimples that make her look like a perennial teenager. "Sounds like it," she said.

"Where are you going next?" Alex asked.

"Probably back to India," Gini said. "I filmed a documentary about an orphanage in New Delhi. I met a little girl there I can't forget. I'm thinking seriously about adopting her, but the Indian government makes it very difficult for a foreigner to adopt one of their children, especially a single woman. I want to see if I can get around their regulations somehow."

"One of my colleagues at the *Times* writes about India. He lived there for quite a while and has lots of contacts. I'll ask him for some information that might help you," Alex said.

Gini's face brightened. "Oh, Alex, could you do that? That would be incredible."

"Would you like a drink?" Alex asked. "We have a lot to talk about."

"Give me a rain check, please, Alex. I'm really tired. We've been here since breakfast, just did a whole performance tonight, and I'm a little jet-lagged. Could we continue this tomorrow?"

"Of course we can. I'd like that very much. Sleep well. You've earned it."

Gini and I headed down the stairs toward our cabins.

"Oh, Tina, he's really interesting," Gini said, seeming to float down the carpeted steps.

"Well, he's certainly interested in you," I said. "And he seems like a really nice guy."

"How old do you think he is?" Gini asked.

"Who cares?" I said. "He's totally compatible."

I could tell it would bother Gini if he were a lot younger than she was. It would never bother me, but things like that matter to Gini.

As we headed to our cabins, we noticed two young men walking ahead of us down the corridor, talking earnestly. I didn't pay much attention to them at first because we could only see the backs of their heads. Then they turned to look at each other and I realized they were Brad and Chef Allgood, who had his arm around Brad's waist. We heard Ken say, "There's more room in my cabin. I have some chilled vodka in my fridge and we can . . . uh . . . talk some more."

Gini and I looked at each other. She saw the worried look on my face.

"Tina. Stop. It's none of our business," Gini said.

"But, he's so . . ."

"It's none of our business."

"You're right. Good night, Gini. I'm going up

to the bar to meet Barry. See you in the morning."

As I headed toward the bar, my phone rang. I saw that the call was from my friend Peter, back in New Jersey.

"Hello, comrade," I said in a thick Russian accent.

"Tina," Peter said. "Is everything OK? I thought you were going to call me when you got to the ship."

Peter Simpson's not a boyfriend, but he likes the same things I do—New York, Cape Cod, everything French, hiking, eating lunch in great restaurants, skiing, dancing. He is divorced and no more eager to get married again than I am, so we have a lot of fun together. He's always available if I need a date for a dinner party or someone to see a play with or go ice skating in Rockefeller Center, or take a boat trip up the Hudson. He's a lawyer who went to law school with my husband and he was a good friend of Bill's. I think he likes to look after me for Bill's sake.

Peter is the brother I've always wanted—or I probably would have fallen in love with him. He's gorgeous—tall, thin, in great shape, still has all his hair, which is gray now. He wears rimless glasses. I'm invariably attracted to men who are smarter than I am—something to do with my father, who was brilliant. I tried to please him all my life, but never could. With the help of a therapist, I've almost managed to stop being hurt that I can never please him, but I still have a long way to go. I don't have to try to please Peter—he likes me the way that I am.

"Everything's fine, Peter," I said, stopping to lean against the wall to talk to him. "I haven't had a minute to call. We just finished our first show and we were a smash hit. There are nice people on this cruise and everything is perfect except the food."

"What did they do, hire a British chef?"

"Exactly!" I said.

"Well, the British know how to do breakfast," he said. "Just fill up in the morning."

"I will," I said. "Don't worry about us, Peter. We're fine. I'll try to call you in a day or two so you'll know everything is OK. What about you? How's the Nelson case going?"

"I'll find out on Tuesday," Peter said. "That's when I'll present my brief to the judge."

"You'll be brilliant," I assured him. "I know how hard you've worked on it."

"Well, maybe," Peter said. "I just want to be sure you aren't planning to run away and join the Moscow Circus."

I laughed. "Tap dancing is enough for me. I'll leave the dare-devil acts to attorneys like you."

"Hah," he said, and I could picture him lifting an eyebrow the way he always does when he's amused.

"Anyway, thanks for checking on me," I said,

remembering that Barry was expecting me to meet him. "It's been a long day. I'd better go. Thanks again for checking."

"Any time, Tina," Peter said. "I miss you."

"I miss you too. Talk to you soon."

Tina's Travel Tip: Not all men who look like Harrison Ford sound like Harrison Ford.

Chapter 5

Add a Russian Accent

Back in the bar, I sat down and ordered a coffee. Three rather sloppy-looking musicians were playing American music on piano, bass, and saxophone. Their music was obviously aimed at the older passengers: "Tea for Two," "Small Hotel." I could have used a little Adele or Van Morrison, a Latino beat, the Stones—anything with a dance rhythm.

Barry hadn't arrived yet. The only other person in the bar was a tall, stunning blond woman sitting by herself at a table near mine. She was wearing a black and white striped top over black pants. Very chic. She smiled and said with a slight Russian accent, "Won't you join me?"

"I'd love to," I said, and took my coffee cup

over to her table. "Hello, my name is Tina Powell."

"I know. I saw your show tonight. I loved it," she said. "I'm Tatiana. When I was younger, my brother and I danced together professionally. Not anymore though. I've turned respectable and teach at the university in Moscow."

"Really?" I said. "How fascinating. What do you teach?"

"Russian history."

"I wish I knew more about it," I said. "Especially now that we're here."

"Come to one of my lectures," she said. "I'm with a British group who hired me to come on this cruise and talk about life before and after communism."

"I'd love to," I said. "Can I bring my gang?"

"Of course." She reached in her oversize black patent leather purse and handed me a copy of her schedule. "Come any time."

I felt a hand on my shoulder and looked up to see Barry standing there.

"Tina, I'm so sorry," he said. "I had to take a conference call from my office. We're working on an antitrust case and I had to talk to the associates who are handling it. It took me longer than I thought it would. One of the hazards of being a litigator"

He held out his hand to Tatiana. "And who is this charming lady?"

"Barry, this is Tatiana," I said. "She's lecturing

to the Brits on this trip. Tatiana, Barry was in my husband's law school class."

"Lovely to meet you," she said and stood up. "If you'll excuse me, I think I'd better turn in. Tina, I hope to see you again tomorrow."

"I'd like that very much," I said, and she glided from the bar on cute beige leather sandals—probably a local acquisition, I noted.

"Interesting woman," Barry said. "Am I too late to buy you that drink?"

"I've switched to coffee—decaf, actually. But I'd love your company. I'm not sleepy—still high from dancing. I'm so grateful to you for showing up when that grimy chef was being obnoxious. Thank you so much for your help."

"I told Heidi about him. I think she'd like to fire him if she had the authority. I strongly suggested she do so."

"Tell me more about you and how you ended up on this ship," I said, taking a sip of the strong coffee, which didn't taste like decaf at all. I'll probably be awake all night, I thought, and then concentrated on Barry.

"It's kind of a caricature of a cruise, isn't it?" he said. "Food you'd send back anywhere else. A crew that never heard of gracious service. A cruise director with all the charm of a traffic cop." I laughed along with him. What a perfect description of Heidi.

"The best part," he said, touching my arm, "is your gang. I still haven't really seen you dance. I saw the beginning—it was great. Then my phone vibrated and I had to take the conference call in my cabin. By the time we worked out all the details, you had finished. I'm glad you're still up." He motioned to the waiter and ordered some coffee.

"Where do you live, Barry?" I asked. "Are you in the city?"

"Yes. Now I am. I used to live in Connecticut when I was married, but my wife got the house and enough money to support her habit of spas, shopping, tennis, lunches in New York, and vacations in Nantucket." He looked grim, but then relaxed and looked at me. "How about you, Tina? Where do you live?"

"In a little town in New Jersey. Champlain. It's a wonderful place. All my friends are there. But I miss my husband." I stopped for a minute and looked into his eyes. They were dark brown, alert and intelligent. "There are so many memories filling that house, Barry," I said. "I'm thinking of moving to Cape Cod so I can watch the ocean whenever I want. There's something about the water that's calming, soothing . . ." I took a deep breath and changed the subject. "It was good to get away for a while and come on this cruise. What made you decide to come?"

"I've been everywhere else," he said, not bragging, just stating a fact. "I went to China last year, so I thought I'd see Russia this time. I'm not sure this is the right way to see it—on this ship, I mean. But I met you, so it's worth the minor inconveniences."

"Thanks. I needed that," I said. And I did need those words of appreciation from a man, I realized.

"I'm sorry about your husband," Barry said, his voice softer. "You must miss him a lot."

"I do," I said. "I especially miss him when I'm on a trip like this. He was always open to new places, new people, new adventures. He would have loved Russia because it's so different from all the other places we went. We can't even read the signs in the towns. Most people don't know much English. It's very different from the European cities we went to."

"Every woman needs a man to take care of her. Look what happened to you with that Allgood guy, that chef."

I stiffened. "I was certainly glad to see you," I said. "I was really scared, but I think it's important for a woman to know how to take care of herself. Otherwise, she's lost when something happens to her man. I'm glad I have a job and the chance to dance on this cruise ship."

"You sound like one of those women's libbers," Barry said, and he didn't mean it as a compliment.

Who said that anymore?

"Yes," I said, "I guess I am."

"You just need a good man in your life," Barry said, taking my hand in his. "Someone to take care of you so you don't have to work or dance on cruise ships. I wouldn't have let my wife do that."

I pulled my hand away. *That's probably why you no longer have a wife,* I thought. I felt icicles forming around the corners of my mouth, but I smiled and said, "Excuse me, Barry. I'm suddenly very sleepy. I think I'll just run along. No—don't get up. Really. I can get back to my cabin all right."

"See you tomorrow, little lady."

Little lady? I left.

Mary Louise was fast asleep when I crept in to the room. The soothing motion of the boat rocked me off to sleep in a few minutes. I dreamed about being in the land of Oz, where all the Munchkins called me "little lady."

Tina's Travel Tip: Bring along some extra cookies in case the chef doesn't show up to make breakfast.

Chapter 6

From Russia With Murder

The next morning, we managed to shower and dress in our tiny cabins. My blue and white striped Brooks Brothers no-iron shirt was as unwrinkled as the day I bought it. Once again, I silently thanked that venerable institution for producing their remarkable blouses.

When Mary Louise, Pat, Janice, and I arrived at the dining room, the place was chaotic. Heidi was running around looking frantic. The waitresses were huddled in a corner babbling Russian to each other. Sasha stood at the door to the dining room and stammered, "Sorry, no food."

"Can you believe this?" Barry said to us.

"What do you mean, no food?" he said to poor

Sasha, who obviously had no idea what was going on.

"Chef has disappeared," Sasha said. "Nobody knows where he is."

"He's probably passed out drunk somewhere," Barry said. "But you can't just say, 'No food,' with all these people expecting breakfast. There must be somebody else who can cook."

He reached out and grabbed Heidi as she ran past, her chestnut hair falling loose from her barrettes. Her brown eyes were crazed and she could barely speak English.

"*Ach*, Mr. Martin. Is *nicht gut*. Vere is dat chef? I spoke sharply to him yesterday because everyone was complaining about the food. Maybe he jumped in river. Maybe he quit and left boat. *Ach du lieber*. He just left. Not one word. Just left."

Barry shook her. "Get a grip, woman! There must be someone in the kitchen, one of the sous-chefs, who can substitute for the chef until you find out what happened to him."

Heidi looked around wildly and saw Tatiana waiting to get into the dining room.

"Tatiana, Tatiana," she called. "Let her through, please."

"What's the matter, Heidi?" Tatiana said. "What's going on around here? Why is everyone running around like scared chickens?"

"The chef has disappeared. No one can find

him. Remember you told me about that young man who is a friend of yours—oh, what's his name?—the Russian, you know, his father owns a restaurant in . . ."

"You mean Sergei? The one who is a sous-chef here?"

"That's his name. Yes. Could you ask him? Do you think he could—"

"I'm sure he could, Heidi. I'll go get him. He refused to go back into the kitchen with the chef in there, but maybe he'll feel more comfortable now since the chef isn't there. I'll see if he's in his room. If he is, I'll bring him back here. Don't worry." She left and walked quickly away from the dining room—this time, wearing red sandals.

"Thank *Gott*," Heidi said.

Alex, the journalist, caught up to us as we headed to a table. He was looking especially attractive this morning, freshly shaven, his blue eyes alert, concerned, wearing a white shirt open at the collar and tan slacks.

"What's going on, Alex?" I said. "Have you heard anything?"

"I don't really know any more than you do, Tina. I saw Heidi with her hair all over the place. She was muttering something like, 'He's gone, he's gone. We can't find him anywhere. Maybe he left the ship without telling me. I don't know what to do.' Then she mumbled something about money being missing. She asked me if I had any idea where Chef Allgood was. Of course, I don't have any more idea than she does."

"Is she going to call the police?"

"The cruise company hates calling the police, but they'll have to. They can't just pretend he hasn't disappeared."

"He probably just left the ship early this morning when it docked," I said. "Why would he stick around here where everybody hates him?"

"There's only one way to get off the ship besides jumping over the rail—the ramp off the main deck. But nobody saw him leave."

In the dining room, people were milling about, not sure whether to sit down or go back to their cabins and search their suitcases for candy bars and cookies.

Gini came in, looking fresh as a daisy in white capri pants and a yellow-and-white striped T-shirt.

"I'm so glad I agreed to come on this ship of fools," Gini said as we sat down at a table near the window. "What's the problem this morning? Is our chef too hung over to make breakfast?"

"Nobody seems to know where he is," I told her. "He's just disappeared. Someone has gone to find a replacement cook for us."

Alex sat down at the table next to Gini, who looked pleased to see him. I hadn't seen her look at a man like that in a long time. A small ray of hope crept into my mind. Could she have found someone she could love? It's always crazy to predict what Gini will or will not do.

Alex said, "Everything's sort of wild this morning. They don't seem to have a Plan B for things like this."

"Tina and I saw the chef going to his cabin with Brad last night," Gini said. "They probably partied too late and they're sleeping it off."

"Sounds logical," Alex said. "If that's the case, I'm sure he'll turn up."

"I hope he doesn't," Gini said. "He's a terrible cook." She turned to me. "So, fearless leader," she said, "what are our chances of getting any food today?"

I never let anything Gini says bother me. I smiled sweetly and said, "Barry has taken over. He has assured us . . . *little ladies* . . . that we will get breakfast today, though it might be a bit late."

"Which 'little ladies' was he referring to?" Gini said, more loudly than she meant to.

I laughed. What had been annoying last night just seemed funny this morning when the whole place was falling apart.

"Relax, Gini," I said. "That's just the way he talks."

"He better not talk about any 'little ladies' to me," Gini said, looking around. "Where is that waitress? I need some coffee."

"This is so weird," Janice said. "My mother

and her friends are always talking about some cruise they've just been on, where all they do is eat. They have bullion and nibblies in the middle of the morning, then some sumptuous feast of lobster and shrimp and oysters at lunch, a mid-afternoon snack, and then high tea—make that super-high tea—in the late afternoon, with pastries and little sandwiches. Here, we can't even get a lousy cup of coffee."

We all laughed. Mary Louise said, "I know what you mean. My aunt was on one of those cruises. According to her, the passengers rest up until dinner, eat six courses, and finally waddle up to the buffet table again at ten for a late-night, stave-off-hunger meal."

"Right," Janice said. "I never heard any of them describe a cruise like this where you have to fight for every mouthful of food, and then it's awful."

We each bubbled over with stories about our own relatives, who described every vacation by what they ate. No tales of whales leaping over the bow of the ship in Alaska. No rapturous descriptions of the quetzals and exotic pink egrets on a Costa Rican cruise. Just mouthwatering reminiscences of chocolate ganache cakes, strawberry shortcakes smothered in whipped cream, and hot fudge sundaes too big to finish.

"They end every story with, 'Of course, we don't eat like this at home!'" Janice said, and we all dissolved into laughter again. We love stories about our older relatives, because they often seem to be having a better time than we are. They travel and eat—the heck with the calories.

"Oh look," Mary Louise said. "Something's happening in the kitchen The waitresses are actually bringing out food."

Olga ran past me. I grabbed her. "Olga, what's happening?" I asked.

"Sergei is in kitchen. He is cooking." She almost smiled. "He makes good food. Wait. You see. What you want?"

"Bring us whatever looks good," Gini said. We sat back and opened our guidebooks, anticipating the day's attractions.

In a few minutes, Olga brought us each a plate with something creamy and fragrant on it.

Gini closed her eyes and murmured "Mmmmmmm" at the first bite of a mushroom omelet, cooked to perfection. Freshly baked croissants nestled on the plate next to the main course.

Heidi, her hair securely fastened in steel barrettes, stopped by our table. Her face looked dark and troubled.

She looked relieved to see the smiles on our faces.

"Is *gut?*" she asked.

"Heidi, this is fabulous," Gini said. Gini never says "fabulous." "Sergei is really good."

Heidi was visibly pleased. "*Sehr gut,*" she said.

"We were wondering about the chef, Heidi," Mary Louise said. "Has he turned up?"

Mary McHugh

Heidi looked out the window and frowned. "Not yet," she said. "But ve are sure he is somewhere."

"Have you notified the authorities?" Alex asked as she started to walk away.

"You mean the police?" Heidi said. "Oh, *ja.* I think someone called them. Do not worry about that chef. That Allgood. He vill turn up." She took a deep breath. As she walked away, she said, "Ve are still hoping ve can go to Kizhi today."

"What's the matter with Heidi?" Gini said after she left. "She's not her usual disciplined self today."

"She's probably worried about her job," Alex said. "But I hope she's right about our going to Kizhi. It's fascinating. The buildings are so old they're protected by the government. The whole location is considered a museum because of the age and value of the buildings. I hope you get to see it, because it's really remarkable."

"Hope to see it?" I asked. "Do you think there's a chance we won't be able to get there today, Alex?"

"I'm afraid so," Alex said. "Once Russian police start investigating something, it could take them all day to find the chef. We won't be allowed to leave the ship until they find him."

"Do you think something happened to him?" Mary Louise asked.

"I don't know, but if he really has disappeared, I don't think anyone will miss him," Alex said.

"Except Brad," Janice said. "I don't see him anywhere in the dining room. If he were here, he would have come over to say hello."

"Probably still asleep," I said. "Don't look so worried, Jan."

"Well, you did say you and Gini saw him going to Allgood's cabin last night, didn't you?" Janice asked.

"They were headed that way," Gini said "And we heard Ken say something about having vodka in his room, but we don't know if they actually went there. Brad could have changed his mind."

"I tried to warn Brad off, because I was really concerned about him," Janice said. "One of the waitresses told me the chef threatened one of the sous-chefs—might have been Sergei—with a knife. I was worried about Brad, so I went looking for him. Just before dinner, I found him out on deck. I told him what the waitress said. He told me the chef went nuts when he tried to work with the kitchen staff, but that this was just an isolated incident. He said he thought the chef was a good person and he was going to have a drink with him after dinner. I told him to be careful."

"When Gini and I saw him last night, he didn't look violent at all," I said. "He and Brad were very chummy."

A loud siren's wail interrupted our conversation and was soon joined by another.

"What's going on outside?" Pat said.

We ran to the deck to find that the ship was swarming with Russian police. The sirens and horns of police boats down below us shattered the stillness of the morning. We looked over the rail and saw that the police were dragging the river. The other passengers were milling around trying to find out what was going on.

"Tina," Sue said, coming up beside us, "what's happening down there?" The painter from Colorado was wearing a long peasant skirt and wide-brimmed hat.

"We don't know, Sue," I said. "We just heard all the noise and came out to see."

"I'm going down there and see if I can find out what's going on," Alex said. "I'll be back."

He was gone about ten minutes. We could see him talking to the police and then he headed back to the ship.

"What did you find out?" Gini asked him.

"The police think the chef was murdered," Alex said. "They broke into his cabin and found it trashed. There was a trail of blood leading to the rail on the deck. They think he was murdered and thrown overboard. I'm going back down there and see if I can find out more. I just wanted to be sure you were all right." He was looking at Gini when he said that. She smiled at him.

As he ran out to the pier at the little island where the Smirnov was docked, we heard a shout from below.

Men from the other boats converged on the spot where the shout had come from. We could see them pulling something out of the water onto the pier. It was hard to tell what they had found.

"Does it look like a body?" Janice asked.

"I can't tell," I told her. "There's too much confusion down there."

One of the men in the police boat turned and waved to a uniformed man who was standing on the deck of our ship.

The man, obviously an authority of some kind, shouted in Russian and ran down the ramp off the ship onto the pier and then onto the police boat. Alex tried to follow him, but the man in charge motioned for him to stay back. We heard Alex shout something in Russian, but the man was kneeling by a lump of what looked like wet clothes, and he didn't answer. There were too many people around what we assumed was a body for us to see what was happening.

"Let's go back in the dining room until Alex comes back," Janice said.

"Good idea," I said. "Want to come with us, Sue? Where's Mark?"

"He's still shaving," she said. "We can't both get in the bathroom at the same time. He'll be along soon. I'd love to come with you."

* * *

The dining room was a scene of total confusion. People moved from table to table asking each other what was happening. One of the waitresses was doing her best to serve everybody at once. She was hopeless. Heidi picked up a tray and helped her.

At a nearby table, Barry was sounding off in his official, jury-addressing voice. "We have a right to know what is going on here. Somebody should make an announcement." He stood up and looked around for Heidi. "You should tell us what protection is provided for us if there is a murderer on board," he said loudly to her. "If anything happens to any of the passengers, this cruise line will have a lawsuit on its hands."

This was a side of Barry I hadn't seen before. His bullying, trial lawyer side. Good thing Bill wasn't here, I thought. He wouldn't have liked Barry at all. And now I knew I didn't like him either.

I'm one of the few people in the world who actually likes lawyers, because I've met so many interesting, civic-minded, generous, brilliant ones. I resent the ones who give lawyers a bad name. Although, I must admit, I do laugh at jokes like: What do you call a thousand lawyers at the bottom of the ocean? Answer: A good start.

Heidi only had to hear the word "lawsuit" once. She rushed over to Barry and tried to calm him down. "Please, Mr. Martin. Everything is under control. Ve don't even know if there has been a murder. The Russian police are very efficient. They will ensure the safety of everyone on this ship."

"You've got to be kidding," Barry thundered. "The chef is missing. The police have pulled a body out of the river. Nobody has seen the chef for hours, and you call that under control?"

Heidi's voice dropped about two octaves. "Please sit down and have a complimentary drink, Mr. Martin. I assure you, everything will be just fine."

I avoided Barry as my gang and I joined Tatiana and some of the British passengers at a table near the window. The Brits looked up as we joined them. They were all talking quietly in a language only they could understand.

"Thisisreallyveddydisturbing," one of the women said.

"Excuse me?" I asked.

"Veddy disturbing," she said into her cup of tea. I realized she was the same woman who wasn't veddy good in the morning.

"Oh, yes, yes, it certainly is," I said, determined not to say anything American.

I introduced my friends to Tatiana, who looked worried.

"Hello, Tina," she said. "What's happening out there? I tried to ask Heidi what was going on, but she's too busy to answer. It looked like they pulled something out of the river. Could you see what it was?"

"All we could see was a bundle of wet rags," I said. "We think it might have been a body. Maybe the chef's body. His room was trashed. Blood all over the place, Alex said. But nobody knows anything for sure."

Alex came back into the dining room and hurried over to our table.

"Alex, what's happening?" Gini asked.

"They found a body," he said. "They think it's the chef because they found his passport in the jacket pocket. It was in a waterproof pouch, so they could still read it. The victim's face is unrecognizable, but he's about the right size for the chef and the jacket was from an English store. I couldn't find out any more than that because they made me leave."

"Didn't you tell them you were from the *Times?*" Gini asked.

"Of course," Alex said, "but that only made them more anxious to get rid of me. I know the inspector, though. I'll see what I can find out from him. I'll let you know."

He squeezed Gini's shoulder and went back outside.

Heidi stopped at our table. "You vant more coffee?" she asked.

"No, we're OK, Heidi," I said. "Are you all right?"

"Hardly!" she grunted. "Two people are missing, somebody is definitely dead, all the passengers have to stay on the ship, and I could lose my job. Everything is definitely not all right. Nothing like this has ever happened to me before. And it's all my fault."

"What do you mean?" I asked. "How could it be your fault?"

She looked around, her eyes darting from side to side. "I threatened to fire Allgood," she said. "What if he did something to himself? Or maybe he drank too much because he was depressed over possibly losing his job and passed out and fell overboard. That would be all my fault."

I put my hand on her arm. "Heidi, you did what you had to do. He was a terrible cook and a terrible person. You did the right thing. Don't blame yourself. And what do you mean *two* people are missing? Who else are they looking for?"

"Nobody has seen that young man, Brad Sheldon, who was with the chef last night. He has to be somewhere on the ship, but no one can find him. He's not in his room. The police are looking for him because he was the last one to see the chef alive. *Natürlich*, they vant to question him. I vouldn't be surprised if he killed Allgood."

"Well, whatever happens, it's not your fault," Pat said. "Don't worry. The police will figure it out."

"Easy for you to say," Heidi said, looking around and then heading for another table.

I took a sip of my coffee, which was way too strong. Seeing Olga passing by, I raised my hand to stop her.

"Olga, could I have some cream for my coffee, please?" I said.

Olga stared at me, uncomprehending.

Tatiana motioned to her and quietly asked her in Russian for the cream. Olga nodded and went back to the kitchen.

"Tatiana, English doesn't seem to be a very popular language over here," Gini said.

"Well, remember, you were the enemy while these kids' parents were growing up. They didn't hear a lot of good things about Americans at home. English is not their favorite language."

"Then how come you speak it so perfectly?" I asked.

"My father loved English. He was a linguist and studied many languages, and he wanted me to love it too. Anyway, English seemed like a very useful thing for me to know. It actually opened up the world for me. I lecture frequently in England and in the United States."

"Tina said you're giving lectures here on the ship," Gini said. "I'd love to hear you."

"You're all invited," Tatiana said. "And, in return, maybe you'll teach me some tap steps?"

"We'd love to," Janice said. "We'll make you an honorary Hoofer and teach you our routines."

"Attention," Heidi said in her loudest, most commanding voice.

We all stopped talking, sure she had something terrible to tell us.

"If you vant," Heidi said, "vun of our guides is giving Russian lessons in library downstairs. Is difficult language, but you might vant to learn. Anyway, starts now."

"Oh let's do that," Mary Louise said. "I'd really like to learn a few more words than *hello* and *good-bye*. Anybody else?"

"Sounds good to me," I said. "And it will take our minds off what's happening on this ship. Let's go."

Tina's Travel Tip: Try to learn a few words of the language of the country you're visiting, in case you need more sour cream in your borscht.

Chapter 7

Privyet, Stranger

As we started down the steps to the library, Janice and Gini caught up with us.

"Where are you guys going?"

"They're supposed to be having a class in Russian now. Want to come?"

"Why not?" Janice said. "All I know how to say in Russian is *da*."

"That figures, Jan," Gini said. "That's all you know how to say in any language. Yes, yes, yes."

"That's better than your *nyet, nyet, nyet*," Janice said. "I have way more fun."

"You're probably right," Gini said laughing. We filed into the snug little library, the shelves filled with books mostly in English. Chairs were

lined up, and we were surprised to see that almost every seat was taken. As we sat down, a large
woman with a southern accent behind us said,
"Have you heard anything about the chef? Is it
true he was killed last night? Was it because of
his cooking?"

"I haven't heard anything," I said, "but I don't
think anyone would kill him for that."

"My husband was ready to murder him after
he ate that terrible dinner," she said.

Elena, a young Russian guide with shoulder-
length blond hair, welcomed us to her class and
stood in front of a blackboard.

"Welcome," she said. "I will give you some simple words and phrases that might be useful. You
can find them later at www.russianphrases.com
if you like. I just want to help you pronounce
them."

She handed out lists of Russian terms to all of
us, in both the Cyrillic and English alphabets.

"One very important thing you must remember," she said, "is that, like many other languages,
there is a formal Russian and a more informal,
more personal, form of address. It's like *vous* and
tu in French, for example. You don't address a
cab driver or a waiter or any stranger with the informal phrase. It's considered rude."

"I don't speak French either," the woman behind us said.

Elena looked puzzled. "That's all right," she
said. "We don't have to worry about French this

morning. We're just going to concentrate on Russian. Let me give you an example of what I mean about formal and informal greetings. When you say hello to a stranger, you use the more formal *zdravstvuyte*."

She pronounced it slowly, something like *zdra-stvoo-tye.*

"If you get to know someone well, you can use the more informal hello, *privyet*"—she pronounced it pree-vyet—"which is the same as 'hi' in English."

She continued down the list of words she had written for us, helping us to pronounce *spa-si-ba* for "thank you," to which you would say *pa-zhal-sta* for "you're welcome," and it can also mean "please." She went on to *proshu proshsheniya*, which means "excuse me"; *Kak dela?* which means "How are you?"; *Menya zovut*—"My name is"; *da-svi-da-ni-ya* for good-bye and finally the very useful *ya budu borscht sbal'shim kalichistvuhm smitany*, or "I'll take borscht with lots of sour cream."

"Ready to try a short conversation?" she asked. We all tried not to catch her eye. I felt like I was back in high school when I hadn't done my homework.

"Come on. There must be one brave soul out there who's willing to try," Elena said.

"Oh what the heck," our Gini said. "Why not?"

"Good for you," Elena said. "OK, you meet a Russian and you want to say hello. What do you say?"

"*Privyet*, stranger," Gini said.

"No, no, too familiar. Class, what should she have said?"

We all looked at our notes and weakly murmured something like "Zdra—stvooy—tye."

"Close enough," Elena said. "I know Russian is a hard language to learn. I just wanted to give you a little push."

"I think we need more than a little push," Gini said. "I think we need a shove."

"So, Gini," Elena said, "what if this nice Russian person asks you your name. What do you say?"

"Meen-ya zovut Gini Miller," Gini pronounced.

"Excellent," Elena said. "See? You're practically fluent. What else would you say?"

"Da-svee-danya," Gini said. "Ta-ta, *adios, au revoir,* and bye-bye. That's it. I think I need to know how to say, 'I don't speak Russian. Do you speak any English?' "

"Good idea," Elena said. "You say, *Vy govorite po-angliyski?* Got that?"

"Almost," Gini said.

Elena soldiered on with "I'm hungry"—*Ya khochu yest*; "I need an interpreter"—*Mne nuzhen pervodchik,*; and she ended with what she said was the most important phrase to know in any language—*Ya Vas lublyu.*

"Anybody want to guess what that means?" Elena asked.

"Has to be 'I love you,' " Janice said.

"Right," Elena said. "How did you know that?"

"She knows it in every language," Gini said. We all laughed and applauded.

"Well," Elena said, "just remember, a smile goes a long way when you don't know the words. That's true in any language."

We thanked her and headed to the Skylight Bar.

"Let's see if there's anything new," Mary Louise said. "It's still a little early for lunch."

We stopped at the table outside the bar where there was always a hot pot of coffee and water for tea, grabbed our favorite drinks, and took them into the bar. Stacy and Andrea were sitting at a table with Pat, who was drinking a glass of clear liquid we knew wasn't water.

"Where've you guys been?" Pat asked. "I couldn't find you anywhere."

"*Prahsteetye*," Gini said. "*Privyet.*"

"Wow," Andrea said. "Where'd you learn that?"

"A guide named Elena gave a class on Russian words and phrases," Gini said. "It was a lot of fun. We learned basic things like 'hello' and 'my name is' and 'I want more sour cream with my borscht.' "

"I wish you had told me," Pat said. "I would have loved to learn some Russian. I don't know any at this point."

"We just kind of went on the spur of the moment, Pat," I said. "Sorry. We should have told you."

"It's OK," she said. "I've been talking to these two and we've been trying to find out what's going on."

"Anything new?" Mary Louise asked.

"Nobody will tell us anything," Stacy said.

"That's because nobody knows anything," Pat said. "The Russians aren't going to tell us, so we just have to wait until they figure out who did it."

"What I don't understand," Stacy said, "is why everyone thinks the chef was such a terrible person." She paused and looked around at us. "Promise you won't tell Nana?" she said.

"Why, Stacy?" Pat asked. "What happened?"

Stacy took a deep breath and then said, "Well, he started talking to me yesterday when I was coming back from the pool in my bathing suit. He was really sweet. He showed me around the kitchen and took me up to the bridge to meet the captain. He was funny and nice. He told me I was pretty. We were out on deck when there wasn't anybody around and he kissed me—he was . . ." She smiled. "It was . . . Anyway, I didn't tell my grandmother about it. He asked me to have a drink with him in his cabin. Nana doesn't even know I drink, so I said no. You won't tell her, will you?"

We looked at each other. It seemed that Chef Allgood's love life was more tangled than we'd realized. We all remembered secrets we kept from our parents.

"No, we won't tell her, Stacy," Pat said. "But I think it's a good thing you didn't have that drink with him."

"Me too! Or whoever murdered him could have murdered me too." She shuddered.

"Stick to dancing, honey," Gini said. "It's a lot safer than drinking with a chef who was probably gay anyway. He certainly seemed to be coming on to Brad."

Stacy drew back in shock. "I don't believe it," she said. "A gay guy couldn't have kissed me like that."

"Maybe he was bisexual," Pat said.

"Is that really possible?" Stacy asked.

Pat looked as if she was going to say more but stopped. This didn't seem to be the right time to go into bi-sexual versus gay versus heterosexual. Way too heavy for a discussion with this sweet seventeen-year-old. Although, these days, she probably knew more than we did.

We watched our teenagers run out of the bar. Pat said, "Come on, let's get one of their crazy drinks—today's special is called Between the Sheets. I asked the bartender what was in it. He looked it up in his little recipe book and said brandy, triple sec, Bacardi, and lemon juice. Want to try one?"

"It's only eleven-thirty in the morning, Pat," Mary Louise said. "And it looks like you've already had a drink. Are you going to have another one?"

"Why not?" Pat said defensively. "We're on a cruise. That's what you do on a vacation."

"It's a little too early for me," I said. "But go ahead if you want one."

"I just might," Pat said, and walked over to the bar.

"Is it me or is she drinking more these days?" Mary Louise asked in a low voice.

"I don't think it's just you," Janice said. "She's always liked a drink, but now—I don't know. Maybe I just imagine it."

"She'll work it out," I said. "Pat is very smart. She'll know when it's time to slow down or get some help. We have to let her get there by herself. She's a therapist, after all."

"I hope so," Mary Louise said, looking over at her friend ordering a drink at the bar. "Sometimes therapists are better at solving other people's problems than their own."

"There's Alex," Gini said, her face lighting up. She waved to him and he joined us.

"Anything new about the chef?" Gini asked him.

"No, now they're concentrating on Brad Sheldon," Alex said, reaching over to take a sip of Gini's coffee. "They're trying to find him so they can question him, but nobody has seen him."

"Do they think Brad killed Allgood?" Janice asked.

"Well, the bartender and Tina and Gini and lots of other people saw them together last night, so it doesn't look good."

"I just can't believe that boy could kill anyone," Janice said. "He seemed so gentle."

"Then where is he?" I asked. "The police must have searched every inch of the ship. He couldn't have gotten off without someone seeing him. You can hardly steal a lifeboat and row away."

"Maybe he jumped overboard and killed himself after he murdered the chef," Pat said.

"Then they would have found his body too when they were dragging the river," Gini said.

"Well, I hope he turns up soon," Janice said.

"Isn't it time for lunch yet?" Pat said, coming back to the table with her drink. "Let's go find out. Heidi said the crew was going to put on a show for us—but not until two o'clock."

We took our usual table by the window in the dining room. It was too early for the rest of the passengers to arrive, but Tatiana walked over to us. She was in her usual black and white: a white silk blouse with tiny gold buttons down the front and tight black pants that showed off her flat stomach and slim hips. "Would you mind if I join you?" she asked.

"We'd love it, Tatiana," I said. "Come sit here next to me."

"Thanks," she said. "I'm feeling a little nervous

because of—you know—because of Allgood. I don't know why they can't find the person who killed him."

"It's not so easy, Tatiana," Alex said. "There are a lot of people who disliked him."

"Enough to kill him?" she asked.

"Well, think about it. Anyone in the kitchen could have finally had enough of his abuse and incompetence and hit him without meaning to kill him. Or Heidi might have underestimated her own strength and knocked him down and killed him. Or Sergei . . ." He stopped, remembering that Sergei was Tatiana's friend.

"Absolutely not Sergei," Tatiana said heatedly. "I've known him all his life. He could never kill anybody."

"Well, I hate to say this, Tatiana," Alex said, "because I know he's your friend. But somebody in the kitchen did hear Sergei say he would get Allgood after the chef pulled a knife on him."

"I don't believe it," she said.

Alex was about to answer when Olga came to take our order. She was actually smiling, and her white-blond hair was swept up in a neat bun.

"How are things in the kitchen, Olga?" Janice asked.

Olga's puzzled expression told us she didn't understand what Janice said. She answered, "Yes. Today caviar with blini for lunch. Sergei fix. Much better."

"Oh, I have to have a couple of those," Mary Louise said. "I love caviar."

We all ordered the blini. While we were waiting, we looked out the window where the police were still dragging the river.

"They must be looking for Brad's body," Pat said.

"Oh, Pat, don't say that," Janice said, tears in her eyes. "I can't bear it if something happened to him."

"You only met him yesterday," said our sensible Pat.

"But I liked him," Janice said. "You can like somebody right away if they're simpatico. Well, I can, anyway. Maybe you can't."

"I didn't mean I didn't like him," Pat said. "I just meant that—oh, never mind."

"Not to change the subject or anything, but do you believe that dead people can send messages to the living?" Janice said.

"Oh yes," Mary Louise said. "The night my grandmother died, I woke up. I knew she was there in that room saying good-bye to me. I don't tell many people about it, because they'll think I'm crazy."

"Why did you ask that, Janice?" Pat said.

"Well, I know this will sound nuts," Janice said, "but last night I had this vivid dream about Brad."

"What was it?" Mary Louise asked, leaning forward.

"I dreamed that he came into my room and sat on my bed." Janice hesitated, looked around. "And Brad said, 'Don't believe anything you hear about me. None of it is true. When you get back home, please tell Maxim that I loved him.' And then he was gone." Janice stopped. "I know it sounds crazy, but I have this really strong feeling that he's dead and he was trying to tell me so."

"I don't think you're crazy, Janice," Gini said hesitantly. "I used to think all that stuff was just mystical thinking, that we make it up to comfort ourselves after we lose someone we love. But then something happened after my father died that made me change my mind." She paused, looking embarrassed.

"Tell us," Janice said. "What happened?"

"Well, my father was a really sensible, down-to-earth kind of person—sort of like you, Pat—"

"Yeah—thanks a lot," Pat said.

"It's not an insult," Gini said. "Cool it, Pat." She took a deep breath and then said, "I loved him a lot. One time we were talking—he was in his eighties then and had some health problems—and all of a sudden he said, out of the blue, 'What if I tried to communicate with you after I die?' I was so astounded to hear him say something like that that I didn't answer for a minute. Then I said, 'What do you mean, Dad?' He looked away and said, 'What if I whistle like I always did when you were a kid when I wanted you to come in for dinner?'

"I was stunned," Gini continued. "I mean, it was so unlike him to say anything like that. Then he said, 'After I'm gone, and you're out here on the porch on a quiet night, and you hear a sound like'—and then he whistled the musical notes C-A-C-F—'you'll know it's me saying hello.'

"Well, I just broke down. I couldn't bear the thought of him not being here anymore. But after he died, wherever I was, I heard those notes when the wind was blowing through the trees. C-A-C-F. I just knew it was my dad saying hello."

She looked up, a shy expression on her face, so unlike Gini.

"I know it sounds like I'm making it up," she said, "but it's so comforting. I love thinking that he's still getting in touch with me."

We were all quiet, hearing those notes in our heads.

"Why not?" Pat said. "You know, one of the laws of physics is that energy cannot be destroyed, it can only be changed. So why couldn't your father's energy live on in the wind?"

"You're right, Pat," Gini said. "Why not?" She smiled at her friend, our mother hen, our wise counselor.

Olga appeared with a tray full of caviar blinis and we took our first bite of heaven. I can take caviar or leave it, and New York blinis are a little heavy. But this dish was light and intense all at the same time, mouthwateringly delicious, but not too sweet. It was just right.

Mary Louise could not stand it one more minute. "Tatiana, could you please ask Sergei how he did this?" she said. "I have to make these blinis when I get home."

"I know how he does it," Tatiana said. "He taught me because my daughters love blinis so much."

"Please tell me," Mary Louise said, taking another bite.

"You have to allow about three hours," Tatiana warned. "Are you willing to spend that much time in the kitchen?"

"I'd spend all day and all night to cook something like this. Go ahead, please."

"I'll write it down for you," Tatiana said. "So you'll have all the ingredients right."

"Tatiana, I love you," Mary Louise said. "I think I'll take you home with me."

"Maybe you should take Sergei, to be sure you do it right," Tatiana said, laughing.

We polished off the blinis and wished we really could pack Sergei in our suitcases.

Mary McHugh

MARY LOUISE'S RECIPE FOR CAVIAR
WITH BLINI

¾ cup buckwheat flour
¼ cup all purpose flour
1 teaspoon instant yeast
½ teaspoon salt
1¼ cup warm milk
2 egg whites whisked until stiff
2 eggs
½ tablespoon sugar
2 tablespoons melted butter

1. Mix the flours together with the instant yeast and salt.
2. Add warm milk and stir until it's smooth. Cover and keep at room temperature for an hour and a half.
3. Add the beaten eggs, sugar, melted butter. Fold stiffened egg whites into the batter. Cover and let stand for half an hour.
4. Cook the blinis the way you cook pancakes—in a frying pan in butter. Use a heaping tablespoon of batter for each blini.
5. Put some cold caviar on each blini, spoon some melted butter over the caviar, and serve sour cream on the side.

Makes 25 to 30 blinis.

Naslazhdaites! Enjoy!

Tina's Travel Tip: If you're bored on your cruise, try to find someone who can do an impression of bacon frying.

Chapter 8

Wake Up and Smell the Bacon

As Olga refilled our coffee cups, Mary Louise smiled and turned to Tatiana.

"Are you going to perform in the show the crew is putting on today, Tatiana?" she asked.

"Actually, I am," she said. "One of the stewards and I are going to do a Russian dance with traditional costumes. Then I'm going to sing a Russian folk song called 'Dark Eyes.'"

"Oh, Tatiana, sing it for us," Janice said. "Please."

"I'll just sing you one verse—I don't want to spoil it for you."

We fell quiet. In a rich full voice, Tatiana

launched into a song so sad and sweet it could only have been Russian. People at the tables near us stopped talking to listen to her.

When she finished singing, we were almost in tears at the beauty of her voice, the sadness of the song.

"That was beautiful," I said when I could speak. "What is the song about? It sounded very romantic."

"That's right, Tina," Tatiana said. "The song is about dark and passionate eyes, the eyes of a lover, the eyes of a brooding dark soul who has captured a woman's heart. She is afraid he will disappear, taking her love and her heart with him."

"Please sing another verse," Janice urged, but Tatiana demurred.

"Ah, no, my friends," she said with a sly smile. "You must wait until our performance to hear the rest."

We all applauded our Russian friend. Tatiana laughed. "Cheer up, my dear Hoofers. Are you going to dance tonight?"

"We're not sure yet," Mary Louise said. "We have to find out from Heidi if she still wants us to perform—you know, because of the police and the investigation and all. Nobody really knows what's going to happen around here. But we're thinking of volunteering Tina to do her impression of bacon frying." She giggled.

"I don't understand," Tatiana said. "What do you mean 'bacon frying'? You have to show me."

"Mary Louise," I said, "I am definitely not doing my impression of bacon frying on a Russian ship. You'd better not mention this to Heidi. I'll kill you."

My friends laughed and all of them started talking at once. "She's famous for this, Tatiana," Mary Louise said. "Come on, Tina. You have to at least show Tatiana."

I shot her a warning glance, and then noticed Tatiana's eager expression.

"OK," I said. "Just this once. For you, Tatiana. But you'd better shut up about this, Mary Louise."

"You know me, Tina," she said. "The Silent One."

"Riiight," I said, shooting her a that'll-be-the-day glance.

I stood up. "You won't believe this, Tatiana," I said, "but I actually did this in public in Scotland. I was there on a Scotch whisky tour—it was a press trip—"

"This was part of your job?" Tatiana asked.

"Yeah," I said. "Rough, huh? The magazine sent me on these trips to recommend them to our readers. Somebody thought it would be a great idea to get the newlyweds soused on Scotch after the wedding."

"What's so bad about that?" Pat asked. "Sounds like the perfect honeymoon to me."

I continued, "We went around to all these different distilleries and had a slight buzz on, by eleven in the morning, from sampling single malt Scotch. I don't even like Scotch, to tell you the truth. But I loved sitting around drinking Scotch in the morning, pretending to be seriously considering the differences among all the kinds they gave us to drink. I wouldn't have known if they were all multimalt Scotch or no-malt Scotch, but I took notes and pretended to be a serious journalist."

"I want your job," Tatiana said.

"The best thing was the party the distillers gave for us the last night we were there," I said. "We danced, sang the Scottish national anthem—they seem to think they'll be free of British rule someday—talked to all the nice Scottish people. I'm of Scottish descent, by the way, and I thought the Scots would be sort of like my father, a little dour, obsessed with golf, sort of distant. Well, they weren't at all dour or distant. They were wonderful, cheerful, joyous people. After they sang and danced for us, they asked us to do something in return."

I stopped. "Are you sure you want me to do this again?" I said to my friends. "Haven't you seen it enough?"

"We can never see it too many times, Tina," Mary Louise said. "Besides, Tatiana has never seen you do this."

"It's that good?" Tatiana asked.

"Wait until you see," Mary Louise said, laughing the way only Mary Louise can, with her whole soul and body.

"OK," I said. "Well, anyway, we all looked at each other, because we couldn't do anything and we weren't prepared. One of the people in our group of writers thought it would be hilarious to announce that Tina Powell would do her impression of bacon frying. If I hadn't had a little—well, a lot of Scotch, I would have melted into a puddle. But, somehow, I went up to the front of this large room in my black and white dress, stockings and heels and pearl earrings, and explained to all these nice Scottish people that I had had a wee dram and hoped they would forgive me for what I was about to do."

"What did you do?" Tatiana said, laughing. "I want to see it."

"OK, but remember, you asked for it," I said.

I lay down on the floor. Fortunately, almost all the other people had left the dining room by then. I remained still for a couple of seconds, and then raised my left arm and wiggled it, then my right arm, next a foot, a leg, another foot and leg, and finally sat up wiggling my whole body like bacon when it is cooking.

My friends have all seen this several times, but they still seemed to find it hysterical. Tatiana laughed so hard, we could see tears in her eyes. She looked at her watch and said, "I'd better go change. I'll never be able to compete with your bacon frying, Tina, but I'll do my best. See you later."

I was still sitting on the floor after Tatiana left, when a familiar voice said, "Ms. Powell, are you all right?"

"Oh yes, Heidi, I was just doing my impression of bacon frying," I said.

"Is that an American custom?" she asked.

"Not really," I said. "It's just something I do after I've had a little Scotch in the morning."

Heidi looked utterly baffled. She muttered something under her breath about crazy Americans and left the dining room.

"It's two o'clock," Pat said. "Let's go up to the bar and see the crew's show. It will take our minds off dead bodies and murderers."

"Let's hope," Gini said.

Every seat in the bar was taken. We stood in the back next to Alex, who smiled when he saw us.

"Sorry I missed your performance of bacon frying, Tina," he said.

"How'd you know about that?" I asked him.

"A totally confused Heidi passed me as I was coming in here. She was shaking her head and saying, 'Bacon frying. She was doing bacon frying.' Gini told me that was one of your many talents. You have to do it for me."

"Watch what you ask for, Alex," I said. "You may be sorry."

The crew appeared, wearing traditional Russian costumes, reds and blues, greens and yellows, with flowers in their hair and smiles on their faces. One of the waitresses was in a red and white polka-dotted blouse tied in front and a black skirt covered with multicolored flowers. Another wore a long-sleeved blouse and striped apron held up with blue and red ties over her white hemmed skirt. It was as if the Russians tried to cheer themselves up with lots of flowers and colors in their clothes.

We hadn't seen much joy from the crew, so it was a pleasure to watch them. They sang for us, while the men did a high-energy dance in which they sat down in midair and then leapt up. Tatiana did a lovely Russian waltz with one of the crew members and sang "Dark Eyes" beautifully, soulfully.

Then Sasha, the wild-haired, wild-eyed dining room manager, leapt onto the stage and said, "I am Sasha. I will sing for you Russian song."

We were expecting a Russian folk song, but Sasha sang us a beautiful sad ballad, in a minor key. We couldn't understand the words, but it brought tears to our eyes anyway. The Russians are really good at sad. Sasha radiated a sweetness that was evident in everything he did on the ship. Although he often seemed overwhelmed, he was always unfailingly polite and kind whenever we asked him for anything.

We applauded and Tatiana hugged Sasha as they all took their bows at the end.

We moved out onto the deck and settled into

brown wooden chairs, which we arranged in a circle. Alex made sure his chair was near Gini's.

"Did you find out anything from the inspector?" Gini asked.

"It was hard to get anything out of him. He said he wanted to ask Sergei more questions. He said Sergei was once arrested for punching someone in his father's restaurant."

"Tatiana never mentioned anything like that," I said. "Are you sure, Alex?"

"I'm only telling you what the inspector told me," Alex said. "I also asked him about Brad Sheldon. He said he's their number one suspect and that it's only a matter of time until they find him. He didn't look all that certain that they would find him anytime soon, though."

"That's crazy," Janice said. "Brad could never kill anybody."

Alex shook his head. "Maybe not, Jan, but the inspector seems to think he could. I asked him where Brad could have disappeared to, and he said he probably sneaked aboard one of the supply boats to go ashore. His body wasn't found in the river and he was not found on the ship. He told me Brad's Russian boyfriend, Maxim, has family members in Moscow. The inspector thinks Brad is probably hiding with them. They're investigating that now."

"Did he mention anyone else who might have done it?" I asked.

"Well, this doesn't really make sense to me, but he did mention Heidi."

"What did he say about her?" I asked, my interest piqued at the mention of Heidi. There was something about her that puzzled me, but I couldn't figure it out.

Alex continued, "I asked him if he really thought she could have done it, and he said, You mean, did *he* do it?' It seems Miss Heidi Gorsuch was originally Mister Gunther Gorsuch. He was head of a boys' school in Stuttgart. When he became a woman, they fired him—I mean *her*—and she took this job as cruise director on our ship. She apparently told one of the crew that Allgood threatened to tell his brother-in-law, who runs the cruise line, that she was really a man, if she had him fired. The inspector thinks Allgood was blackmailing Heidi. She could have killed the chef—she's strong enough."

My earlier observations of Heidi's large feet and deep voice suddenly took on a whole new meaning.

"I asked him how Allgood could have known that," Alex said. "The inspector shrugged and said, he must have found out somehow. You must admit, Heidi doesn't look like your typical woman."

I was so flabbergasted, I couldn't reply.

"Do you buy any of this, Alex?" Gini asked.

"I don't know what to believe at this point,"

Alex said. "I never heard anything before about Sergei or Heidi. I did think Brad must have had something to do with the murder since he was the last one seen with Allgood. Anyway, I don't know who did it, but you should all be careful. Don't go anywhere alone. OK?" He put his arm around Gini.

"We'll be fine, Alex," Gini said, leaning against him. "Don't worry."

But we were all worried. I couldn't shake the uneasy feeling that whoever killed the chef was still on the ship.

Tina's Travel Tip: A fur hat with a hammer and sickle pin probably isn't a good gift idea for a Wall Street lawyer.

Chapter 9

Nesting Dolls and Fur Hats

"What do we do for the rest of the day?" Gini asked. "I want to go on shore and see some more of Russia. That's why I came on this trip in the first place. I want to photograph that little town we can see from here. What's the name of it, Alex?"

"Kizhi," he said, giving it its Russian pronunciation, Kee-zhee. "You really should see it. It's very old, all wooden buildings. You can buy fur hats there too."

"Oh, Alex, do you think you could get permission for us to go there?"

"Let me see what I can do," he said, and left to find Heidi.

He was back in ten minutes, smiling. "Come on, Hoofers. Heidi arranged for Andrei, our guide, to take you and the rest of the passengers to Kizhi. She said it would be easier for the police to search the ship if we were all off the boat."

He looked at Gini. "Mind if I come along?"

"I'd love it," she said. "But won't you be bored? You must have seen it a million times."

"I won't be bored," he said. "I can't imagine ever being bored when I'm with you. By the way, your show was awesome last night. You should wear those rain slickers all the time."

Gini laughed. "Glad you liked them. Incidentally, how old are you? Just asking."

"Forty-eight," he said. "Just telling. Hope that's not too old for you."

"I'm fifty-one," Gini said. "I hope that's not too old for you."

"I always say, it's not the number of years we've lived that matters. It's what you learn along the way that counts. Besides, I've always been attracted to older women," he said, smiling. "You can teach me whatever I need to know."

"I don't think there's much I could teach you," Gini said, grinning wickedly. "But I'll try."

We filed out to the pier, where we could see the town of Kizhi, now classified as an outdoor museum because of the ancient wooden buildings preserved there. This was entirely different from the other small villages we had seen. There were no red and blue and yellow domes dotting the island, just dark wooden buildings with white domes above the trees.

We joined our guide, a large unsmiling Russian, impatiently waiting for the rest of the passengers. His round, mustached face was shaded by a white cap pulled down to his eyes. He wore a red, thigh-length loose vest over a white dress shirt with a red and blue striped formal necktie. He carried a paddle with the number twenty on it, which he held up.

"I am Andrei," he said when we had all gathered around him.

He didn't seem particularly thrilled to be ushering a group of mostly Americans around an island he had visited hundreds of times. "I will be your guide for today's tour. Today, I show you very old buildings, very important historically. Please keep moving. Do not stay in one place too long. Look for number twenty, which I hold up if you get lost."

I was standing closest to him. "Are we still on the Volga River?" I asked.

"No," Andrei said. "This is Lake Onega, the second largest lake in Europe. And this island is unique. Is kind of open air architectural museum with buildings from the thirteenth century and churches built by Peter the Great in the eighteenth century."

We moved in closer to hear him.

"You will see many beautiful things," he said. "Because there are so many ancient buildings, this island is protected by UNESCO as a World Heritage site. The buildings are mostly made of wood, so there is always danger of fire."

He pointed to a large boat anchored on the lake. "That is fireboat, ready to put out fires if they occur. Many of these buildings have not been adequately maintained. There is fear they will decay and be destroyed in the next ten to fifteen years if something isn't done to preserve them."

He walked us to a massive wooden building and opened the door. "Come, we go in old farmhouse, where fifteen people lived with their animals."

We followed him into the house, which had an earthy smell due to the dirt floor on the lower level. "This part of house was the barn," Andrei said. "Cows and horses and chickens lived here. The warmth from their bodies heated whole place. Is very cold here in winter—many times it was seventeen degrees below zero on your Fahrenheit scale. No central heating in those times, so farmers glad to have animals indoors for heat. We go upstairs where people lived. Come."

We climbed the stairs to a large room, where the family would have done everything—made the pots that cooked the food that they grew, created fabric using wool from the sheep they raised, dined and read and studied. There was a large loom on one side of the room with a vividly colored cloth woven in bright blues and reds and pale yellows. Nearby, a blond, sweet-faced woman sat in the corner in traditional Russian dress—a white blouse with a dark blue apron covering her long, light blue skirt. She was mending clothes. Near her a cradle hung on a wooden arm suspended from the ceiling. It was cleverly designed so the baby could be moved to whatever part of the room the mother was working in.

At another table, a dark haired, slender woman was working with beads on a tray making earrings, necklaces, and bracelets. She looked up and smiled as we walked by. Snuggled next to her on her chair was a little tortoiseshell cat, who woke from her nap to watch us with luminous green eyes.

"Do you speak English?" Pat asked the woman.

"Oh yes," she said. "For tourists. Many American or British."

"Would you mind if I petted your cat?" Pat asked, stopping to kneel next to the cat, really just a kitten.

"You can pet her, the woman said. " You like cats?"

"Oh yes," Pat said. "I have a cat named Eliza. She's a tortoiseshell too, just like yours. I miss her."

"This one Sophia. So sweet. Good company for me."

"I know," Pat said. "Eliza is sweet too. She

113

sleeps on my bed at night and bumps her face against mine in the morning when she sees that I'm awake. When I come home from work at night, she runs to the door to say hello and I pick her up for a hug. I don't know how I ever got along without her. I love her. May I?" And she reached down to pick up the kitten.

"She like that very much," the lady said, smiling.

Pat cuddled the cat close to her chest, rubbing her face against its soft fur. The kitten purred loudly in Pat's arms.

"Sophia easy for me to take care of," the woman said, " I am often here. She comes with me. I don't want to leave her at home. She is no trouble. Just goes in box, eats when hungry, and sleeps next to me here. Not even get scared when visitors come. " She smiled at Pat. "She likes you."

"I inherited Eliza," Pat said. "I didn't want a pet. Didn't even like cats very much. Then one of my clients was moving away and asked me if I would take her. I said I would and she's been the joy of my life ever since."

Sophia purred even louder.

"I always think cats look like they're smiling when they purr, don't you?" Pat said.

"Oh yes," the lady said. "Smiling at you."

Pat didn't want to leave, but Andrei was urging us along for the rest of the tour.

"Good-bye, little cat," Pat said, returning the kitten to her mistress. "Stay warm."

"Imagine fifteen people in here every day, all year long," I said to Pat. "I've had days when I went nuts with two kids and a husband in the house."

Andrei overheard us. "The women did get out of house," he said. "Besides picking crops in the field, it was their job each day to load horses and cows into boats and take them to the grassy meadow across the lake so the animals could graze. At end of day, the women went back to get animals and bring them to house for the night."

"And I complained when I had to pick up my kids from soccer practice," Mary Louise said.

"Me too," I said. "We had it easy."

Andrei led us down a ramp from a door on the top floor. We left the house and walked toward a strange-looking church, also made of wood. I had never seen as many domes on one church as there were on this one. They were all made of a light-colored wood. I strained to hear Andrei describe it.

"This is Church of the Transfiguration," Andrei said. "Built in 1714, also of wood and without a single nail. Not one nail in whole building! Church has twenty-two wooden onion domes made of aspen. Too cold for services in wintertime, so people built smaller church nearby called 'winter church,' which could be heated by fire. Now is one priest who comes to island. In winter he must come by helicopter because water is frozen and no boats can come through."

Gini said, "Be right back," and ran down to the lake to photograph the curve of the shoreline along the island's edge. Alex followed her and held her bag while she took pictures.

"Check out Gini and Alex," Janice said to me in front of the church as we waited for the others to take pictures. "He follows her around like a little puppy dog."

"I think they really like each other," I said. "I've never seen Gini so lively or so happy."

"Was his information about India helpful?" Pat said.

"Yeah, what's happening with that?" Mary Louise asked.

"The Indian government is giving her a really hard time," I said. "But Gini just adores this little girl and is going to keep trying. I'm sure Alex will help her. *The New York Times* can do anything."

"He seems like a good guy," Janice said. "Do you think he's right for Gini?"

"Who knows who's right for Gini?" I said. "She's always so quick to find faults in a man. Maybe she's not meant to be married. Not everyone is."

"Tell me about it," Janice said.

"Oh, Janice," I said, "I meant to ask you, did you find Brad yesterday? I know you wanted to talk to him more about that play he's in."

"Yes, I saw him a couple of times, because I wanted to keep him from going to Allgood's room. The bartender told me that Brad and the chef had a drink at the bar last night, and he said he heard them say they were going back to the chef's room."

"Gini and I saw them heading for Allgood's cabin," I said, pulling Janice along to catch up to Andrei. "Did the bartender hear anything else they said?"

"Well, his English isn't all that good," Janice said, "and they talked too softly for him to hear much. But he said they kept touching each other and, once, they kissed. He said—remember, he's Russian and Russians aren't all that cool with gay guys—he said, 'Disgusting. Men not born to love men. Should only love women.' "

"Our country's getting better about gays, but it wasn't really all that great until very recently," Pat said.

I knew that Pat often counseled gay couples in her practice. "It's still hard for gay couples who come to see me," she went on. "They often have a really tough time in the community, especially if they are bringing up a child. Why do some straight people go bananas if gay people get married? How does it hurt *them*? I just think of

117

their children. It would be so great for those kids if gay marriage was legal all over the country."

"Yeah, gay people should have the same chance to be miserable as the rest of us," Janice said.

Pat laughed, and said, "It doesn't make sense. I'll never understand it."

"Explain this to me, Pat," I said. "How could that chef be kissing Stacy one minute and Brad the next? Do you think he swings both ways?"

"Well, some people do," Pat said. "But I don't think Ken was bisexual. I think he wanted something from Brad and he was pretending to be gay."

"What do you think he wanted?" I said.

"I think he was using him to get to New York," Pat said. "Maybe Brad changed his mind and wouldn't help him, and they got into a fight, and one or both of them got killed."

"Could be. Who knows what happened. Oh look, Andrei is motioning to us to follow him."

We caught up to Andrei and followed him on a tour of the rest of the island, past a windmill on a base that rotated so that the blades always faced the wind, and past many pale domed churches. We stopped in front of a small church that looked like the poorer sibling of all the other impressive churches we had seen. It had one dome on top.

"This is Church of the Resurrection of Lazarus, built in the fourteenth century," Andrei said.

"Bible says Jesus raised Lazarus from dead. He was dead four days and Jesus made him live again." He shrugged. It was obvious he didn't really believe this story, but it was part of his spiel. "Believe what you like."

Andrei smiled and bowed to us. "This is end of tour," he said. "I hope you enjoyed. The rest of the day you do as you like. Many beautiful things for sale here."

He pointed to the tents lining our path back to the ship. "You can find presents to take back to your family and friends. Ship will sail through some beautiful lakes. You can see more little towns."

I walked past the row of tents and saw merchants selling everything from fur hats to Russian nesting dolls. The passengers from our ship crowded into the small shops, looking for gifts for their loved ones. Russian dresses and scarves hung on display, creating a rainbow of color and beauty.

"Look, lady, you like this one," a young man called to me as I passed his booth. He held up one of the nesting dolls, called *matryoshka*, which had Putin as the largest doll. When I stopped, he opened the doll and showed me Medvedev inside Putin, then Yeltsin inside him, then Gorbachev, then Stalin, and, finally, the smallest doll was Lenin. I considered getting one just to prove I'd been to Russia, but changed my mind.

I walked along the path, glancing at all the

119

goods in each tent, some things really beautiful, some junk. There were fur coats, colorful Russian dresses striped in blue and yellow and red that I loved but knew I would never wear at home, costume jewelry that was pretty but not my style. I'm not a shopper, but I kept looking for something to take back to my daughters and grandchildren.

I poked around until I saw a table in one of the tents with the most exquisitely decorated eggs I had ever seen. I mean real eggs, not the Fabergé kind. I don't know how, but some gifted artist had painted a little scene or design on the outside of the egg, then made a small hole in the bottom of the shell, drained out the contents, and attached a thin silver cord to the top, making incredibly beautiful Christmas tree ornaments. Fragile, delicate, something I could only buy here. Perfect for my daughters.

The man who owned the shop watched me as I looked at his goods. "All original," he said. "Very good souvenir for you."

Each egg was different. Each one perfection. I wanted to buy them but I was worried they wouldn't make it back to New Jersey in one piece.

"Can you pack these so they won't break on the plane going home?" I asked. "They look so fragile."

"Of course," he said. "We make sure your eggs arrive safe. Do not worry."

I carefully picked up an egg that was white

with a black design, the silhouette of Santa Claus in his sleigh sailing over the rooftops of a city. His reindeer kicked up their hooves, and some toys stuck out of his bag in the back. The reins he held, the runner on the sleigh, the tiny chimneys on the buildings were all exquisitely painted with precision and care. It was hard to imagine an artist who could have a touch delicate enough to produce something so intricate on an eggshell without breaking it. I was enchanted. My daughter Kyle would love this one.

I looked at the other eggs, all of them beautiful, until I found one that would be just right for my other daughter, Laurie. It had holly branches decorated with red ribbons and gold bells painted on it. Each of these eggs was like nothing I had ever seen before. I knew my daughters would appreciate their uniqueness.

The owner of the shop wrapped each one painstakingly, securely, so they each had a good chance of getting back home in one piece.

I was ready to go back to the ship, but the last tent I passed had a table piled high with fur hats. I couldn't resist trying some of them on. One was a small tower of light gray Persian wool. Another was a white ermine beauty that covered my whole head. There was a dark mink band that looked really good with my blond hair.

The man behind the table said, "You should wear hats. You have beautiful face."

Listen, I know my face isn't beautiful, but it's

not bad. My blue eyes are my best feature, but I also lucked out with a Scottish complexion of pink and white, a not-bad nose, and a good smile.

I tried on several more round fur hats. Then I saw a large one made of mink, with a hammer and sickle pin on the front. Peter would love it. Solid, respectable lawyer that he is, he still enjoys shaking people up once in a while. I think one of the reasons he likes me is because I do too.

"I'll take this one," I said.

Tina's Travel Tip: When buying gifts in Russia to take back home, remember that a foot-high samovar is hard to pack.

Chapter 10

Samovars and Underwear

None of my Hoofer pals had made it back to the ship yet. They were all still raiding the tents. I knew it would be a while until they got back. Unlike Gini and me, they actually liked shopping.

I ordered a cup of tea in the Skylight Bar and was enjoying being alone when my phone rang. It was Peter.

"Hi, beautiful," he said. "I just wanted to find out how everything is going. How's the ship? Are you a huge success? I've been waiting for you to call me."

"I'm sorry. Peter, listen—now don't get upset, but there was a murder on the ship."

"Are you kidding? What do you mean, don't get upset? Are you all right? What's going on there? Who was murdered?"

"We're all right. The British chef I told you about—the one who was a terrible cook—someone killed him."

"Do they kill people in Russia for being terrible cooks?"

"I hope not or I'm next," I said.

"You're not a terrible cook," he said. "You just don't think cooking is an art form."

I couldn't help it. Murder or not, I had to laugh. Peter can always make me find humor in any situation. It's one of the reasons we're such good friends.

"Really, Tina. If there's a murderer running around loose on that ship, I wish you'd come home."

"I figure as long as I don't cook anything, I'm safe," I said, and we both laughed again.

"Seriously, Tina, be careful, will you? I don't want anything to happen to you. What's going on now?"

"The Russian police are going to ask us some questions."

"Don't give them anything but your name and social security number," Peter said, sounding like the defense lawyer he once was when he worked for Legal Aid, before he joined a law firm. "Just remember, SOS in Morse code is dot-

dot-dot dash-dash-dash dot-dot-dot, in case you meet the murderer."

I laughed. "Who knows Morse code anymore? What are you—eighty years old? Anyway, I'm innocent. I didn't kill him even though the food was really bad. Stop worrying about us and tell me how you're doing. How was your day in court?"

"It was postponed, yet again," he said. "I'll be glad when I can stop practicing my argument and actually give it."

"What about the Chinese opera? How was that?" We'd gotten tickets together, but after the Hoofers were booked for our Russian cruise, I encouraged Peter to go with another friend.

"Oh, fine, I suppose," he said. "I think Elizabeth enjoyed it more thanI did. All those high sopranos got on my nerves after a while."

I remembered Elizabeth, an attractive associate at Peter's firm, whom I'd met at their Christmas party. To my surprise, I felt a twinge of jealousy.

"I'll call you after they question us so I can tell you about the Russian interrogation techniques," I said. "I hope there won't be any waterboarding."

"You always say you're going to call," Peter said. "And then you don't. I'm warning you, I'm going to keep bothering you if I don't hear from you."

"Oh, Peter, wait—there's something I want to ask you. One of your classmates from law school is on the ship. A man named Barry Martin. Do you know him?"

Peter said, "As a matter of fact, I do. I never liked him. He tends to throw his weight around a lot. But maybe he's changed. He's a partner in a Wall Street firm."

"I don't think he's changed. There was something about him I didn't like, so I'm relieved to hear you didn't like him either. It's not just me."

"No, it's not just you. But seriously, Tina, call me, will you please? Give me an update. If the murderer is still on the loose, he might strike again."

"I will, Peter. Stop worrying. We're fine. Bye."

I didn't really believe the "fine" part. The idea of a murderer lurking around the ship somewhere was always in the back of my mind, no matter how hard I tried not to believe it.

An hour later my friends came rollicking into the Skylight Bar, carrying paper bags full of gifts to take home. They were all giddy with the fun of finding treasures they couldn't buy in New Jersey.

"What did you guys get?" I asked. "Gini—you're empty-handed. Couldn't you find any tourist traps to raid?"

"I'm like you. Not a shopper," Gini said, "as

you well know. But I got some pictures of the churches and the river that are gorgeous. Look, I'll show you."

She opened her digital camera and showed me photos of cathedrals taken from unusual angles, and of Russians selling their goods. The women wore scarves around their heads—babushkas, they called them—and long dresses that were blue or red or green or yellow. Their bright garments were flashes of light against the gray buildings, like the domes of the cathedrals that brightened up the sky that day. Another photo showed a man playing music on a tray of glasses filled with water at different levels. Gini had captured the uniqueness of the little town. The shots couldn't have been taken anywhere but Russia.

"Oh, Gini, they're beautiful," I said. "Can you send them to my phone?"

"Sure. Just tell me the ones you want," she said. "But when I get home, I'll edit my photos and post the best ones on my website. Then you can download any that you like."

"Tina," Mary Louise said, reaching into a shopping bag, "look at these black lacquer boxes. I bought one for everyone for Christmas presents. Aren't they lovely?"

She pulled out a shiny black enamel box with a painting of a sleigh drawn by three prancing steeds, one red, one white, one beige. A young couple rode in the sleigh and the driver was urging the horses on, waving his arms. It was night-time, with stars and a crescent moon in the sky. The wind was blowing the horses' manes. You could feel the movement and urgency of the scene.

"It's gorgeous, Mary Louise," I said. "I love it. They'll be great gifts. Hope I'm getting one."

"If you're good," she said. "I don't suppose you bought anything, you anti-shopper."

"Wait till you see," I said. "I actually broke down and bought something I couldn't resist for Laurie and Kyle. I'm dying to show you, but they're super breakable and they're already wrapped for the trip back home. So I'll show you when we get back."

"What did you buy?"

"They're hard to describe but . . . they're eggs decorated for Christmas. They're so beautiful I hate to give them away."

"I saw those in one of the tents," Janice said. "They really are gorgeous. I wanted to buy some to take back, but I was sure I'd break them."

"The man promised me they would survive the trip," I said. "I mean, he does this all the time."

"Good luck with that," Janice said.

"Looks like you got something big, Jan," I said. I could hardly see her over the top of the bag on her lap. "What is it?"

"I couldn't resist it," Janice said. "It's just so . . .

so . . . Russian." She carefully pulled out a large samovar.

"Oh, Janice, that's really beautiful," Pat said. "But how will you get it home? I mean, how will you get it in your luggage?"

"I'll worry about that later," Janice, our impractical Hoofer, said, holding up a blue and gold samovar over a foot high. It was a large coffee urn, with two sturdy gold and black handles on the side, a little gold tap in front, and a scene painted all around that would remind Janice of this trip to Russia every time she looked at it.

The scene showed a white-bearded man wearing a red-belted coat with a fur collar. He was using a wooden stick as a cane as he stood sturdily on the snowy bank of a small lake. Next to him were three birch trees, black and white against the blue sky. Behind the old man was a young woman wearing a red jacket over an orange dress which was partly covered by a green apron. Her head was covered by a yellow babushka and she was carrying two baskets suspended on a wooden rod across her shoulders. Way in the background was another warmly dressed woman walking her dog. While it was unlikely that anybody would ever actually make coffee in this work of art, it would be a perfect addition to Janice's apartment, which was filled with unusual acquisitions from her travels and from the plays she'd appeared in.

"I'm coming for coffee as soon as we get back home," Mary Louise said to her, and opened another bag she was carrying.

"Tina, you have to see this fur hat I bought for Sam," she said. Sam is her youngest son. "Can't you see him wearing it at college?"

"It'll probably end up on your head at a cocktail party," I said. "They're incredible though, aren't they? Here's the one I got for Peter."

"You got Peter a hat with a hammer and sickle on it?" she said, laughing. "He'll never wear that."

"You don't know Peter," I said. "He just seems conservative. He tries to be sensible and proper, but when you give him a little push, he can be persuaded to do anything. You'll see. He'll wear this hat to court one day."

"I keep telling you," Mary Louise said, "you should marry him."

"Stop pushing Tina to get married," Janice said to Mary Louise, frowning at her. "Let her alone. She'll get married again when she's good and ready—or not. Right, Tina?"

"Right," I said, looking at my watch. "Probably at half past never. I'll never find anybody like Bill again. Hey, it's 6:30, girls. No time for dinner. Let's just get some appetizers and a glass of wine here, and get dressed for our performance. "

We nibbled on some blinis, some eggs stuffed with salmon caviar, some sauteed shrimp, and a yummy salad, and headed for our rooms, laden with our shopping bags and carefully wrapped gifts.

Mary Louise and I took turns dressing in our narrow cabin. We were going to wear our Judy Garland outfits—black silk tuxedo jackets with black and white camisoles underneath, black stockings, and black tap shoes.

"Are you nervous, Tina?" Mary Louise asked.

"Not really," I said, and realized I wasn't. "We've done this so many times before. And, anyway, I've given up getting nervous. My attitude is, *I'm doing my best for you, and I know you want to like us.* You're not nervous when you get out there, are you? You sure don't look it."

"Well, sometimes I am, but I know what you mean. It's fun doing this." Mary Louise paused for a second, a guilty look on her face. "You're the only one I'd say this to, Tina, but I like getting away from George once in a while. No meals to fix, no house to clean, no complaints to listen to. I love him, but some of my happiest times are away from him. I always feel I'm not living up to his expectations."

I've never understood how such a terrific woman could stay married to a grouch like George, but I keep my mouth shut. If she gets fed up enough, she'll leave him. Only she can make that decision.

I put on my makeup. My motto is less is more,

131

but I tried to make my eyes look bigger, my cheeks rosier, and my lips glossier. I often remember how easy it was when we were Andrea's and Stacy's ages. All you had to do was stand there. Now, we have to try a little harder. My hair will stay blond until I tell it not to. And it helps that—with a lot of work—my body is still slim and firm. And we all have great legs. Of course, black stockings make them look even better. Fifty is the new thirty, I reminded myself with a wink at the mirror. Then, I sat on the bed to give Mary Louise her turn to primp.

At nine o'clock, all the chairs were filled in the Skylight Bar.

Heidi stood center stage and drew herself up to her full six feet, two inches to speak to the crowd.

"I haf the great pleasure of presenting the famous Happy Hoofers from America who will knock your socks off," Heidi said, smiling at her mastery of the English language, "with their vunderful dancing. Please give a varm velcome to the Happy Hoofers."

The grumpy old man looked as if he was trying to smile, and actually clapped with the rest of the audience. We had converted him into one of our fans—or at least into someone who didn't hate us.

Gini pushed the PLAY button on our CD player

and we took our dancing feet to Forty-second Street, flapping, ball changing, scuff heeling, lunging, and kicking up our heels, flaunting our beautiful legs for all to see, on the Volga River on the way from Moscow to St. Petersburg. *Ypa!* as the Russians would say. Hooray!

The gentleman in the front row sat up straight when we danced onto the stage in our short jackets and black stockings. His eyes opened wide and he clapped along with everybody else when we finished the first number.

We smiled, bowed, and march-stepped into "Boogie Woogie Bugle Boy from Company B," ending with a rousing "Tap Your Troubles Away."

The place exploded with cheers and cries for more, more, more.

We thanked them and worked our way back to our cabins, ready for bed and whatever would happen the next day, which turned out to be not at all what we were expecting.

Tina's Travel Tip: A few laps around the deck early in the morning is good exercise on a cruise ship—unless someone is chasing you.

Chapter 11

What's Behind Door Number Two?

When I woke up the next morning, it took me a minute to remember where I was and that somebody had been killed on this ship and nobody knew where or who the murderer was.

I pulled my notebook out of the drawer and started to write my "morning pages." It's something I do every day. I guess you could call it a kind of meditation. A writing meditation. I love the quiet, the feeling that it's a new day and anything can happen.

I started writing my thoughts every morning

after Bill died. It seemed to help. I got rid of all those nattering, chattering complaints and whining. It was a way to clear my mind for the day, leaving it open to creative ideas, new experiences.

When I first started my morning pages, I would write about missing Bill, or about my mother and how she didn't have a clue about what I really cared about, or my children's failure to call me. Gradually my left logical brain switched over to my right creative brain and I began thinking of new ways to get where I wanted to go.

It was my way of getting to the heart of whatever was most important that day. I really needed it on that ship. As I wrote, I tried to think of all the people who could have killed Ken Allgood and to figure out where Brad Sheldon had disappeared to. Did Heidi kill the chef so he wouldn't reveal the secret of her gender change? Did Sergei want Allgood's job so badly he murdered him for it? Did Brad kill him and get off the boat somehow? Or did he witness Ken's murder and also get killed by the murderer? If that was the case, where was Brad's body?

As I was writing down my thoughts, someone slipped a piece of paper under our door. I picked it up and found a notice from Heidi.

Attention, all passengers. We must ask you to stay on the ship today while the police investigate

135

*the death of Chef Kenneth Allgood. Please report
to the Skylight Bar at ten A.M. to meet with the
police inspector, who will ask you a few questions.
As soon as he has finished his interviews, the
ship will sail to St. Petersburg and you will be allowed to go on shore for a tour of the city. We
apologize for this inconvenience. All drinks for
the rest of the cruise are complimentary. Again,
we apologize for this unexpected turn of events.
Heidi Gorsuch, Cruise Director*

Time for a couple of laps around the deck. I
put on my running clothes and shoes and
sneaked out of the cabin, leaving Heidi's notice
for Mary Louise to find when she woke up. It
was a cool, clear morning and once again I was
glad we were in Russia in June. People were already on the banks of the river fishing. A couple
of them waved as our ship glided by. The land-
scape was dotted with multicolored onion domes
in every town. Not just solid-colored domes, but
striped ones, and some even decorated with stars
or diamonds.

There weren't many people on deck. Just a
few dozing in wooden chairs, waiting for the dining room to open. As I was starting my third lap,
a man with gray wispy hair and uneven teeth
caught up to me.

"I say," he said, "do you know what's going on?

I can't find out anything because everybody is speaking Russian."

I realized he must be one of Tatiana's group of Brits.

"Someone seems to have murdered the chef," I said, amazed that this man didn't know that.

"Oh, too bad," the man said. "His meals were so good."

"Well," I said, "His breakfast wasn't bad."

"Will there be breakfast this morning?" he asked, looking worried.

"I'm sure there will be something to eat," I said. "Did you get the announcement about the Russian inspector questioning us in the Skylight Bar this morning at ten?"

"There was a piece of paper on the floor when I left the cabin, but I just assumed it was about laundry or something," he said, stopping to pull his socks up out of his shoes.

"No, no, it's important," I said, jogging in place while he struggled with his feet. "The inspector wants to ask us some questions."

"I say," he said, looking as if he had discovered the answer to all his questions. "Is this one of those mystery cruises? Will Inspector Morse turn up? Did you know his first name was Endeavor?"

"Really?" I said, trying to follow this non sequitur. I tried to think British. "His name was Endeavor Morse?" I asked. "Did they call him Dev? Endy?"

"Just Inspector Morse," my British companion said, starting to run again. "He never told anybody his first name."

"I'm afraid it's not a mystery cruise," I said. "Too bad. That would have been a lot safer. No Inspector Morse. We're going to be questioned by a real Russian inspector. There was a real murder with a real body and they're trying to find out who did it."

"Bother!" he said, and ran on ahead of me, his shoelaces untied, his socks bunched up in his shoes again. I knew I shouldn't laugh, but I couldn't help it.

"What's so funny?" Gini said, running up next to me with Alex by her side.

They were obviously together and I knew they didn't just meet on deck for a run. Something about the way they looked at each other, the way their arms touched, the happiness on Gini's face, made me think their friendship had moved up a notch.

"Good morning, you two," I said. "I just had a British moment. You're up early. Hope you slept well."

"We didn't do much sleeping," Gini said.

"Oh?" I said, pretending to mind my own business.

"We were talking about the murder most of the night," Alex said, not looking at me, his eyes on Gini.

"Did you solve it?" I asked.

"Well, we really wonder about Brad," Gini said. "I know it seems unlikely that he could kill anyone, but no one has seen him since the chef disappeared."

"I just can't believe that Brad would do it, Gini," I said. "I think he left the ship and the police can't find him."

"Then who do you think did it?" Alex asked.

"I think it was Sergei," I said. "He hated Ken and wanted the chef's job himself. Janice told me that Ken pulled a knife on him one time, and Sergei might have decided to retaliate later on. I'm going to ask Tatiana what she knows about him. What do you think, Alex?"

"It might be Sergei," he said, his expression conveying his doubt. "But I keep remembering what the inspector told me about Heidi. Remember, he said that she used to be Gunther Gorsuch. And he also said that Allgood threatened to tell people she used to be a man if she fired him. Heidi could have decided to get rid of him because of that. She'd be strong enough to strangle him and throw him overboard."

"I forgot about that," I said. "It's possible, I guess, but Gini's probably right. Much as I hate to believe it, the most logical suspect is Brad Sheldon. He was the last person seen with the chef. By the way, did you get a note telling you to come to the Skylight Bar at ten this morning?"

"Yes, and I know that inspector," Alex said. "His name is Ivan Gregarin, and he has a solid reputation. I've interviewed him for the *Times* often. He's very smart and very thorough. It will probably take him several hours to question us. He's a former KGB guy. So don't count on seeing St. Petersburg today. Let's go shower and get some breakfast."

"See you later, Tina," Gini said, her face radiating happiness.

I envied them. Bill and I used to look at each other like that even after almost thirty years of marriage. I knew what he was thinking. I could see the love in his eyes when he came home at night—and he *always* came home at night. He wasn't a cheating kind of man. We had a date every Friday all the years of our marriage, when we went into New York for dinner and a foreign movie. We always made sure to hire a babysitter and keep our date, even when the children were little. It lit the spark again and made us realize how much we loved each other and enjoyed being together. We never ran out of things to talk about.

I wanted that feeling again— part old shoe, comfortable, lived-in, and part sex and laughter. I wanted him back so fiercely it was like a sharp pain, like a deep, empty place in my gut. I wanted his arms around me. I wanted to talk to him, play with him, make love to him. I wanted him back.

I crave excitement, adventure, a little danger. It doesn't seem fair to have the desires of an eighteen-year-old in the body of a fifty-three-year-old woman. But there it is and I'm not giving up.

I headed for the door that opened onto the stairs leading down to my cabin and tried to open it. It moved a little but something was blocking it. I couldn't open it all the way. I thought I heard a groan, but I couldn't be sure. I yelled to Alex and Gini, who were leaving the deck and heading toward their cabins. They heard me and came back.

"What's the matter, Tina?" Alex asked.

"It's this door," I said. "I can't get it open. Something or someone is blocking it. I thought I heard a groan."

Alex pushed against the door with his shoulder and it opened a little more, just enough for us to see the legs of a man lying on the floor.

"Wait here," Alex said. "I'll go through the other door and come back."

Another moan came through the door from the man lying on the floor just a foot or so away from Gini and me on the deck. We both tried to shove the door open but it wouldn't move. In less than a minute, Alex was next to the man.

"Come around the other way," he said to us. "I don't want to move him. Looks like he's been shot in the head."

"Who is it?" Gini said.

"I can't tell because he's face down. He's still groaning, though. You'd better go and get help. Find a doctor and tell him to get here fast."

Gini and I ran through the other door and found Heidi going down the stairs to the dining room.

"Heidi," I said, "Quick. Get a doctor. Hurry. A man's been shot on that stairway off the deck. Hurry up. Alex is with him. He's still moaning."

"*Gott in Himmel,*" Heidi said. "*Ach du leiber!*" She ran off to get a doctor.

Gini and I ran to find Alex, who was kneeling beside the victim.

"It's Sasha," he said when he saw us. "Did you get a doctor?"

"Heidi's getting one now," Gini said. "Is he still alive?"

"He won't be much longer, even if that doctor gets here right away," Alex said, his hand on Sasha's wrist. "I tried to ask him who did it, but he just kind of gurgled something. I couldn't understand him. He was shot close up, but he's got some hair under his fingernails. They can do a DNA test and find out who shot him."

Heidi came running up to us with one of the passengers on the ship, a thirtyish woman I'd seen swimming in the pool with her two young children. "I'm Dr. Bennett," she said in a crisp British accent. "Stand aside, please."

We moved back to let her through. She knelt beside Sasha, felt his wrist, then looked up with a serious expression.

"Get the police," she said. "Tell them there's been another fatality."

"Sasha," Heidi said, bursting into tears. "Oh, Sasha, vy did he have to shoot you? You didn't do anything."

"He must have bumped into the murderer unexpectedly and whoever it is shot him," Alex said. "That means he's still on this ship."

Gini and I stumbled back to our cabins to tell our friends what had happened. The five of us perched tightly on the beds in Gini's room, our knees nearly touching each other.

"That's it!" Janice said. "I'm not hanging around a ship that has a murder a day. How do you know we won't be next? Tina, let's get off this crazy boat now and go home. Even if they don't give us our full fare back."

"I agree," Mary Louise said. "This is getting way too weird. Why would anyone kill Sasha?"

"Maybe he found out something he wasn't supposed to find out. Or he saw something he shouldn't have seen," Pat said. "But let's not rush off the ship. Let's at least hang around to see what happens next."

"Pat's right—"

"Well, I'll stay until I get some breakfast," Janice said.

I knew that meant she would stay for the rest of the trip.

"First things first," Gini said. "I need a shower. See you in the dining room."

Tina's Travel Tip: A cruise is not a good place to count calories. Change your mantra to eat, eat, eat!

Chapter 12

How's Your Pojarski?

I stood in line at the buffet table and looked around at the young Russian waitresses lined up at their stations, ready to serve coffee or tea or hot chocolate. They were in their usual disorganized condition, with worried looks on their faces.

"Good morning, Olga," I said to our server. "Are you all right?"

"Is true?" she asked. "Sasha is dead?"

"I'm afraid so, Olga."

She covered her face and ran back into the kitchen.

Tatiana came in and joined me at the buffet table. She was wearing a bright red top with black pants. As usual, she was a vivid, dramatic contrast to the rest of us dressed in pastel shirts and blouses.

"Tina," she said, "I heard there has been another murder. That Sasha, poor Sasha, was killed."

"It's terrible, Tatiana," I said, sipping my cocoa. "Alex and Gini and I found him after our morning run. He was lying at the top of the stairs."

"This is getting really bad," she said. "What are the police doing, anyway?"

"I guess we'll find out later on," I said. "The inspector is supposed to ask us questions at ten. I have a few questions I'd like to ask him."

"Come sit with me," Tatiana said. "My Brits aren't all that talkative in the morning."

I joined her at her table with the Brits and said hello to a middle-aged, pinched-faced woman looking down at her plate. "This certainly turned out to be an exciting cruise, didn't it?" I said. "Who would have expected one murder, to say nothing of two?"

"Mmmmppphhhmmph," she said.

"Excuse me?"

"I don't usually . . . uh . . . talk this early," she said in a muffled voice.

"Oh, sorry," I said. I didn't tell her she forgot to button her blouse.

"Excuse me, Ms. Powell," Heidi said, stopping by our table. "Are you all right? Such a shock this morning. Poor Sasha."

"Oh, Heidi," I said, "what's happening? Do they know who shot Sasha?"

Her eyes filled with tears. "No, I can't imagine why anyone vould vant to kill such a sweet man. He never said a cross word or did an unkind thing to anybody."

"I understand the inspector is going to question us this morning," I said.

"Ja," Heidi said. "This is very difficult for the passengers, so Sergei says he vill give cooking demonstration for anybody who vants to vatch him. Vould be good distraction, I think."

"That's a good idea, Heidi," I said. "Why don't you announce it here? People are totally freaking out. This will give them something to do while they're waiting for the police to question them."

Heidi stood up and in a loud voice told the assembled crowd about Sergei's offer.

After breakfast, several women in the crowd joined Tatiana and me as we headed into the kitchen. My gang joined us.

"This is really nice of Sergei," Mary Louise said to Tatiana. "In the middle of all this chaos, he's going to give us a cooking lesson. That's so great."

"Sergei is fine young man," Tatiana said.

Gini poked me without saying anything, but I got her message: Maybe fine, maybe not.

About twenty of us crowded into the small kitchen where Sergei was waiting for us. His white jacket was clean, his dark hair neatly tucked under a cap. He spoke in halting English and Tatiana filled in the words he didn't know.

"Good morning," he said. "I make for you Chicken Cutlets Pojarski. Big favorite in my country. Tatiana, you could tell history of these cutlets, please?"

Tatiana smiled at the group and said, "Long, long ago, in a little town called Torjok, there was a tavern where everybody came. The man who owned the tavern was named Pojarski. He invented this dish, which was originally made of chopped game and beef, and formed into cutlets. Now it's usually made with chicken and served with a paprika sauce. Sergei will show us how he makes it. He's made it for me many times and it is really delicious."

"OK," Sergei said.

He took a mixing bowl from the refrigerator.

"In this bowl, I have been chilling for several hours chicken cutlets which I ground up and seasoned with salt and pepper, nutmeg, and melted butter. Now I take the cold meat and make first a ball and then flatten out into a cutlet."

"How much butter, Sergei?" Mary Louise asked, taking notes.

"About six tablespoons," Sergei said.

"Fat city," one woman in the crowd muttered.

"Is not diet dish," Sergei said, and we all applauded him. "Food should not be punishment." We clapped again.

"So," Sergei said. "You put flour on piece of waxed paper. Next to that, eggs mixed with corn oil and water in a glass dish. Over here at end, you put panko crumbs on large dish. Panko better than bread crumbs because lighter." He looked at the lady on a diet and said, "Fewer calories." She smiled.

"Take chicken cutlets," he continued, "put first in flour, then in eggs, then in panko. Put in refrigerator for a short time while you make paprika sauce, which is what makes Chicken Pojarski different and so good."

"So far, it's just like the chicken cutlets I make at home without calling them Pojarski," Mary Louise said to me in a low voice.

"Well, let's see what he does with the sauce," I said. "That's what makes it a pièce de résistance."

"Tina, you know I never give up," she said.

"OK," Sergei said. "Sauce. Also not diet," he said to the butter-resistant woman.

"First, you chop some onion and cook in butter. Then add paprika, flour, and thyme, and stir, stir, stir. Put in chicken stock. I make from chicken bones, but you can buy in supermarket. Not as good, but OK. Use whisk and stir in stock.

"You, lady," he said, pointing to Mary Louise. "Come, pour in stock and stir for about three minutes while it simmers. Don't stop stirring. Is what makes it good."

Mary Louise, who was loving all this, moved to

the stove next to Sergei and whisked and stirred the mixture while he beamed.

"You have made sauce before?" he asked her.

"Not like this, Sergei," she said. "But I'm cooking this one as soon as I get home."

"You have husband who like Russian food?" he asked.

"He likes every kind of food," she said, "as long as he doesn't have to do anything but sit down and eat it."

"You like cooking every night?" Sergei asked.

"Not really, Sergei," she said. "But I love him so I cook for him."

"Lucky man," Sergei said, and we all applauded again.

"OK. Now I show you best part. Again, not diet food. I add to this sauce stirred with special touch of lady who loves husband, heavy cream, and make boil. Careful, so does not—how you say it, Tatiana?"

"Curdle, Sergei," Tatiana said.

"Yes, curdle. Then add lemon juice—about two teaspoons, not too much—more salt and pepper, and the best part, a little cognac. But wait, not finished yet. You add a lot of butter," he looked up at the lady again. "Sorry. But is necessary. Add butter and finally about a quarter of a cup of sour cream. Bring almost to a boil, but do not boil, or will . . . curdle," he looked up triumphantly.

We all applauded, including the low-fat lady,

and he said, "I put sauce in little dishes so you can taste." He passed them around to all of us.

"This is to die for, Sergei," Mary Louise said. "I love this."

"Is because *you* stirred in chicken stock," Sergei said, smiling at her.

"I don't think so," she said. "Can't wait to do this at home for George."

"Maybe when I get my restaurant in St. Petersburg, you will bring him for Cutlets Pojarski."

"I'd love to, Sergei," she said, adding in a low voice to me, "but I like my cutlets without dead bodies."

MARY LOUISE'S RECIPE FOR
CHICKEN POJARSKI

2 skinless, boneless chicken breasts
¼ to ½ teaspoon nutmeg
10 tablespoons butter
½ cup flour
1 large egg
1½ teaspoons corn oil
1½ tablespoons water
1¾ cups panko crumbs

1. Chop or grind chicken. Add salt and pepper, and nutmeg. Melt half the butter and add to mixture. Mix thoroughly and chill in the refrigerator.
2. Shape the chicken into small cutlets and dip first in the flour, then in the egg combined with the oil and water, and then into the panko. Put in the refrigerator briefly.
3. Sauté the cutlets in the other half of the butter until golden brown and serve with paprika sauce.

Paprika sauce:

2 tablespoons butter
3½ tablespoons chopped onion
2 teaspoons paprika
1 tablespoon flour

½ teaspoon thyme
½ cup chicken stock (canned is fine)
½ cup heavy cream
2 teaspoons lemon juice
1½ teaspoons brandy
¼ cup sour cream

1. Cook onion until transparent in half the butter in a saucepan. Add paprika, flour, and thyme, and stir. Add chicken stock or canned broth, and simmer for three or four minutes.
2. Add heavy cream and heat until just boiling. Add lemon juice, salt and pepper, and the brandy. Stir in the remaining tablespoon of butter and the sour cream. Heat until just boiling, but don't boil.

Makes two mouthwatering, very filling portions.

Priyatnogo appetita!!! Bon Appetit to you!!!

Tina's Travel Tip: If there's a murder or two while you're on your cruise, don't complain to the cruise director. She might be the killer.

Chapter 13

Just Your Name and Social Security Number

On the dot of ten, Heidi and a man in uniform came into the Skylight Bar, which was filled with passengers. The man's dark eyes scanned the room, moving from person to person as if he could read our minds. He was tall and thin with a military bearing.

The lounge grew quiet as Heidi picked up a microphone.

"Do not be alarmed," she said. "Inspector Gregarin would just like to ask you a few questions."

She handed the microphone to the inspector, who blew into it, creating an ear-splitting screech of feedback, before he cleared his throat and spoke.

"Thank you, Miss Gorsuch," he said. "Ladies and gentlemen, we were sent here to find some information about the murder of Kenneth Allgood, who was the chef on this cruise. Now it seems we must also ask you if you know anything about the death of your dining room manager, Sasha. We retrieved a body from the river yesterday, and we have reason to believe it was Mr. Allgood. We won't really know until we have done further tests, but his passport was found on the body. Then, this morning, someone shot Sasha. We're hoping one of you might have seen something that will help us. I would like to ask each of you a few questions out on deck, so it will be private, and then you will be free to go back to your cabins. Please excuse this inconvenience. We will make this as fast as we can. Thank you for your help." Looking at the microphone as though it were a snake that might bite him, he handed it back to Heidi.

One by one, the inspector escorted the passengers and the crew to the deck and spoke to them, seated on one of the wooden chairs. I couldn't hear his questions or the answers, but I could see the interrogations from my seat near the window.

He started with Sergei. After a few questions, I could see the sous-chef shouting at the inspector. Red-faced, he jumped up so violently, he knocked over his chair. Tatiana, watching from a chair near me, ran out on deck. She said something to Inspector Gregarin and then put her hand on Sergei's arm to calm him. She spoke again to the inspector, who dismissed Sergei and then questioned Tatiana.

When he was through with Tatiana, she followed Sergei back to the kitchen. Gregarin motioned to Barry Martin to come out on deck. He strode out to confront the inspector, who asked him a question. Instead of answering, Barry pulled out his cell phone, dialed a number, and began to talk, totally ignoring the inspector. Gregarin waited several minutes for him to put down his phone, getting angrier and angrier. He finally motioned to one of his officers to escort Barry off the deck. Barry tried to pull away and ignore the officer, but was taken back to the Skylight Bar, his phone still against his ear. The inspector clearly was not pleased.

Heidi was questioned next. We could see her talking earnestly, gesturing with her hands, standing up and sitting down, obviously very nervous and upset.

The inspector took Heidi's hand in his and turned it back and forth, examining her knuckles and wrist, tilting her head to look at her

Adam's apple. He pointed to her foot and she took off her loafer. He looked at her ankle and foot and then handed her shoe back to her. She stomped her foot into it, shouting so loudly that we could hear her through the window.

"Vat are you doing? I had nothing to do with this. I have nothing hidden in my shoe. Do you think I hide a gun in there? *Ach!* I never should have hired that chef. He was a terrible cook. You should have eaten some of his food. It vas terrible. And Sasha was like my own son."

The inspector motioned again to the police officer, who accompanied Heidi off the deck. She came into the bar, still talking loudly.

"He made me take off my shoe," she said. "Why vould he do that?"

The bartender came over to her, put his arm around her, and led her out of the room.

I turned back to see what would happen next. The inspector talked to each of the waitresses one by one. They still remembered stories their parents told them about police interrogations when the Communists were in power. Even now the country was run by an ex-KGB officer, so they were terrified. It had never been a good thing to talk to the police in Russia.

After he finished with the waitresses, the inspector saw me watching and motioned to me to come out on deck.

"You are Ms. Powell? One of the entertainers?"

"I am," I said.

"And it was you who found Sasha this morning?"

"Yes, my friends and I found him."

"What time did you find his body?"

"About six-thirty, I think."

"What were you doing up at that hour?"

"I usually go for a run early in the morning."

"You have trouble sleeping?"

"No, no. I sleep well. But I only need about six hours' sleep. Then I'm awake and ready for a run."

"You are not worried about anything?"

"Only the usual things."

"What do you mean—the usual things?"

"Are our costumes ready for the evening performance? Will we remember the routines? Will anybody else be killed on this cruise? You know, stuff like that."

"Do you find homicide funny, Ms. Powell?"

"Of course not!" I said heatedly. "I just don't know where you're going with this line of questioning, Inspector."

"Did you hear any gunshots while you were running?" he asked.

"No," I said, "or I would have called somebody right away."

"Was anybody else with you on that run?"

"Just one of the British passengers and my

158

friends Alex and Gini," I said. "I'm sure they didn't hear anything either or they would have done something. Sasha must have been shot before any of us went out on deck."

The inspector paused, put on his glasses, and looked at the notes in front of him. "Did you know the chef?"

"I only met him a couple of times, very briefly," I said with a grimace.

"You did not like him?"

"No, I didn't."

An alarm went off in the back of my mind. I heard Peter's voice clearly: *"Tina, just give your name and social security number. Don't volunteer any information you're not asked for. It could come back to bite you."*

The inspector looked at me over the top of his glasses. "Why didn't you like him?"

"He was a—he was—he couldn't cook very well."

"So you wished him dead because of his cooking?"

"No, no, of course not," I said, stammering. "I didn't say I wished he were dead. I just wished we had another cook on the ship, that's all."

"Isn't it true, Ms. Powell," the inspector said, speaking slowly, "that Mr. Allgood attacked you on deck on your first day aboard this ship? That he tried to rape you after you complained about his cooking?"

Whooooa, I thought. How did he know about

that? Barry maybe. Or Heidi. *Does he think I killed that little fink? Watch out, Tina.*

"He was just obnoxious, Inspector," I said, working to keep my voice steady. "He didn't try to rape me. Thanks to Mr. Martin, I got away from him."

"But you were happy when he was replaced by another chef?"

"Well, I—uh—I—," I said. "The food was much better when Sergei started cooking."

Inspector Gregarin wrote for several minutes in his notebook. I kept thinking of Peter Falk as Columbo and how he always borrowed a pencil from someone and scribbled away in his notepad when he was talking to people, and how all those scribbled notes led to the murderer. I could just imagine the inspector jumping up and announcing to the other passengers, *"We have found the woman who murdered Kenneth Allgood."* Then he points a finger at me and says, *"It was Tina Powell."*

"Do you know anything else about Mr. Allgood that might be useful?" he asked.

I examined my nails, which could have used a good buffing. "Well, I did hear that he threatened some of the workers in the kitchen with a knife. They were all afraid of him. Some refused to go into the kitchen with him after that."

"Who told you that?"

"One of the waitresses told my friend," I said.

"Which friend?"

"Janice Rogers."

The inspector said something to the police officer in Russian. The officer went into the bar and brought Janice back with him.

"May I go, Inspector?" I asked.

"No, please stay. Would you repeat what you just told me?"

"You mean that the chef threatened some people in the kitchen with a knife?"

"Yes, and when I asked you how you knew that, you said that—"

"A waitress told me that, Inspector," Janice interrupted. "And I told Brad Sheldon."

"Why did you do that?" the inspector asked.

"I was worried about Brad, so I went looking for him. Just before dinner, I found him in the corridor. He told me he thought the chef was a good person at first because he wanted to visit Brad in New York. But then he talked to some people in the kitchen who said he had a knife. That scared Brad. He was going to talk to the chef after dinner and ask him if that incident really happened."

"What was your relationship to this Brad Sheldon?"

"I met him on our first day aboard the ship. He told me he was an actor, that he had seen me act in a play. He asked if I could help him with a part he was going to play in New York. I promised to help him, but I never got the chance. Do you have any idea where he is now, Inspector?"

He ignored her question and fixed me with a

piercing look. "I have a few more questions for you. Please wait inside, Ms. Powell."

I joined my friends while the inspector talked to Janice. She came back in after a few minutes and said, "He wants to ask you some more questions, Tina."

"What did he ask you, Jan?" I asked.

"All kinds of questions about Brad: If he was gay, how long did he know the chef, if I knew him before I got on the ship, if I had a lot of gay friends, if we all had husbands. He even asked me about my daughter! He knew all about her. He asked me if I took drugs too." She shuddered. "He sounded as if he had already made up his mind that Brad had killed the chef. But I know that Brad could never kill anybody. He must be hiding somewhere, scared to death."

"I wish he'd get this over with," I said, and went back out on deck again.

"Are you almost finished with me, Inspector?" I asked. I forced my voice to remain steady.

"Just a few more questions, Ms. Powell." He looked down at his notebook and then asked, "What do you know about Tatiana? Is she a friend of yours?"

"I met her on this cruise and she's a very fine person. She's a professor at the university in Moscow and highly respected in her field."

"But it is my understanding that she was responsible for getting Mr. Allgood into trouble."

"No, she just helped Heidi get a new chef

when Mr. Allgood disappeared. She knew one of the sous-chefs and recommended him."

"Hmmmm." The inspector wrote three pages of notes. They were in Russian, of course, so I couldn't even read them upside down. I was getting nervous. Now it looked like I had implicated Tatiana and maybe Sergei in the chef's murder.

"This German woman—Heidi?" the inspector asked. "She wanted to get rid of the chef too?"

"Well, she wanted to replace him," I said, "not get rid of him. It looked like Sergei would be a good replacement, since he knows the restaurant business. His father owns a restaurant in St. Petersburg. He knows how to cook Russian food." My babbling wasn't helping anybody.

"We have reason to believe that Miss Gorsuch was once a man named Gunther. Do you know anything about that?"

"I heard something about it, but I don't really know whether it's true or not. Look, this is only our third day on this ship. We don't know any of these people well."

"What about your friend Barry Martin, the American tourist? Would he have any reason for wanting the chef dead?"

"Of course not! He's a highly respected lawyer in New York."

"Did he threaten Mr. Allgood when he found him attacking you on deck?" the inspector asked.

"He just told the chef to leave me alone," I said.

"Or—?" the inspector said, and he obviously knew the answer.

"Or he'd break both Allgood's arms," I mumbled, looking down at the deck.

Inspector Gregarin took more notes. I wished Peter were there. Or at least Columbo.

The inspector looked up. He cleared his throat.

"What about your friend, Alex Boyer, the bureau chief for the *The New York Times*? I understand that he intervened in a quarrel between one of the waitresses and the chef. He told Ms. Gorsuch that the chef should be fired."

"A lot of people said they wished the chef would be fired after eating his food, but that doesn't mean they would kill him. Everyone hated that man."

Gregarin glanced at his notes again and changed direction.

"We have reason to believe that Mr. Allgood was a homosexual. Was that your impression?"

I was getting exhausted, so I answered more angrily than I meant to.

"You can't tell if a person is a homosexual just by looking at him," I said. "I have no idea whether he was homosexual, bisexual, heterosexual, or no-sexual. What kind of a question is that?" I stood up and started to walk away.

"Sit down, please, Ms. Powell," he said, and

wrote furiously in his notebook. I sat down on the edge of the deck chair. Another ship passed us going in the other direction and gave two loud blasts of its horn to greet us.

The inspector frowned at the interruption, then said, "The bartender said Mr. Sheldon had a drink at the bar with the chef, Mr. Allgood, two nights ago, and they left together. What do you know about Mr. Sheldon? Did you ever see him lose his temper, make angry gestures, threaten anyone?"

"No, of course not. He is a very mild-mannered, gentle person."

I stood up again. I'd had enough. "The only angry person I've seen on this whole ship was Mr. Allgood," I said. Now, if you have no further questions—"

"Not right now," he said, "but please let us know if you hear anything about Mr. Sheldon. We haven't been able to locate him. You may go."

I stumbled back to the bar and collapsed at one of the tables. My friends surrounded me.

"Are you all right?" Janice asked.

"No, I'm not," I said. "I haven't done anything, but I feel guilty of something. I'm not sure what."

"I know what you mean," Janice said. "That man makes you feel like you must have committed some crime, or at least you know who did it."

"Who did what?" Alex asked, joining us again.

"The inspector sounded like he thought Brad

was the killer," I said. "I know you think he is too, but I still don't believe it."

"He certainly seems to be a prime suspect," Alex said. "Let me talk to the inspector and see what I can find out. I might be able to pry something out of him. I'll be back."

A loud voice broke into our conversation. "I'll have that man fired," Barry said. "He talked to me as if I killed that stupid chef. I don't know who he thinks he's talking to, but I'm calling the State Department. He can't get away with this." His voice got louder as his anger mounted.

My friends looked at me. He's your problem, their expressions said, do something about him. I got up and put my hand on Barry's arm.

"He made all of us feel guilty, Barry. As a trial lawyer, you must know that's his job. To find out information. To get us to say things we don't want to say. Try to calm down and get some lunch. I'll see you later."

"He won't get away with this."

He walked away, his face angry and red. There was a long silence. Then Pat said, "Tina?"

"Don't worry," I said. "I'm trying to get rid of him as fast as I can."

"Too bad," Mary Louise said. "He does look like Harrison Ford."

"Harrison Ford or not," I said, "he's got to go."

Tina's Travel Tip: Always travel with Lysol.

Chapter 14

Surprise Party!

After lunch, I walked down the stairs and along the corridor to my room. As I put the key in the lock, I heard the door of one of the cabins open behind me. For some reason, I felt the hairs rise on the back of my neck. I turned to see who was there. A hand covered my mouth and I felt a hard object against my back.

"Quiet," a deep voice said, "or you're dead."

I felt myself being shoved into my cabin and pushed down on Mary Louise's bed. My assailant slammed the door and grabbed my wrist with a gloved hand. The grip was so strong, surely this was a man, and a powerful one. His face was completely covered with a brilliantly colored Russian scarf—except for his eyes, which were darkly menacing. He was pointing a gun at me.

"We leave ship now," he said, his voice muffled by the scarf. His accent could have been Russian or almost anything else. His voice was gutteral, harsh.

"You my . . . how you say?—hostage."

I tried to stall him. "Why me?"

"You famous. They let me go if you with me."

"No, no, I'm not famous. They won't care. You'll never get—"

"Shut mouth," he said, jabbing my rib cage with his gun. "Get up. We go."

I felt something hard underneath me on the bed and realized it was a spray can.

Hearing a noise outside the cabin, he looked away for an instant. That was all the time I needed to pull out the can of Lysol I had been sitting on and spray it in his eyes. He yelled and fired the gun but missed me. I sprayed again and tugged frantically at the door of the cabin. It wouldn't open. I kept spraying. He shot again but he couldn't see. I crouched down so he would miss me.

The door opened suddenly, and I ran out into the arms of a Russian police officer. He must have heard the gunshots. The officer grabbed me away from the line of fire as my assailant kicked the door closed.

The policeman shot through the door with a

volley of bullets. Hearing no answering gunfire, he flung open the door. The window was smashed and the guy was nowhere in sight. The inspector appeared, gun drawn, and found me sitting on the floor of the corridor, shaking.

"You are all right?" he said.

"No," I said, gasping for breath. "I'm . . . I'm . . ."

"Who was it?" he asked.

"I don't know," I said. "He had some kind of accent. A Russian accent maybe but I'm not sure."

"Was it Brad Sheldon?"

"No—Brad Sheldon is American. I told you this man had a Russian accent. And he was bigger, stronger, I think."

"You did not recognize his face?"

"It was covered with a scarf."

"What kind of scarf?"

"Bright colored," I said, struggling to talk. "Like Russian women wear. Red and orange and yellow and blue."

"Could you see his hair?"

"No. That was covered too."

"But his voice was high, or deep or . . . ?"

"His voice was deep and he had this accent and . . ." I was shaking all over.

My friends came running in, crowding the hallway.

"Oh, Tina, what happened?" Mary Louise said. "We heard shots. Are you all right?"

"Your Lysol saved my life!" I exclaimed, drawing worried looks. My friends thought I had lost my mind until I filled them in.

"Inspector," Gini said, "did you catch him?"

"No, he escaped, but we will find him. He cannot get off this ship."

I couldn't stop shaking. "It was . . ." I couldn't talk. "He was . . ." I took a deep breath. "He said he was going to use me as a hostage to get off the ship because he thought I was famous. I don't know where he got that idea. I'm not even famous on this ship. No one has ever pointed a gun at me before—I was sure he was going to kill me, and you know what I thought?"

"What, honey?" Pat asked.

"I thought, I'll see Bill again." Tears flooded my eyes.

My friends hugged me. Once again, I wondered what I would ever do without these women.

"I'll always be all right as long as I have you four," I said, sniffling.

"Let's get a drink," Pat said. "I think we all need one."

This time I had to agree with her. "Great idea," I said, and I tottered off to the bar with my friends holding me up.

Tina's Travel Tip: If you don't know what else to do, tap dance.

Chapter 15

One Desperatador, Please

The Skylight Bar was full of people who had heard several different versions of my story. They asked if I was all right, if it was true that I captured the guy by myself, if I had been shot in the shoulder but not badly hurt, if the police had taken the murderer off the ship.

I told them what really happened.

"You mean the killer is still somewhere on the ship?" Sue asked.

"I'm afraid so," I said. "But there are police everywhere. They're checking every inch. They'll find him."

My teeth chattered. I didn't really believe what I had just said. Just in time, the bartender handed me a tall glass of pink, fizzy liquid. I lifted it and took a tentative sip. It was sweet, soothing . . . I took another sip.

"Ms. Powell," a man said to me, "I am a doctor. One of the passengers on this ship. I heard you were hurt. May I have a look at your wound?" He opened his medical kit.

"Oh, I'm not shot," I said. "He missed me. I'm fine—just a little . . . uh . . . gun-shy."

I convinced him I was not bleeding anywhere, and he left.

"Tina, tell me everything that happened," Alex said, sitting down next to me. "Are you all right?"

"Not really, Alex. Having a gun pointed at you is definitely not fun." I told him the whole story. He said I would be on the front page of *The New York Times* the next day.

"I've always wanted to be in the *Times*—but for something I wrote, not for Lysol spraying an assailant," I said.

Heidi ran up to me and took my hand. "Ms. Powell, thank *Gott*, thank *Gott*," she said. "I'm glad you're all right. You are so brave."

I took another gulp of the cocktail and felt the room tilt a few degrees.

"Good heavens, what's in this?" I asked.

"Tequila, triple sec, grapefruit juice, honey, and—vat is that other thing?—oh, *ja*, grenadine," Heidi said. "Ve call it the Desperatador."

"Please to listen, ladies and gentlemen," said the Russian inspector's voice over the loudspeaker. "We ask everyone to stay in the Skylight Bar until further notice. We will tell you when it is safe to leave."

"This is an outrage," a loud voice said. "I have an important phone call to make from my cabin. They can't make us stay here."

"I'm afraid they can, Barry," Alex said. "I wouldn't try to leave here if I were you. You might be the next one at the wrong end of a gun."

"They're a bunch of incompetents. They couldn't find that killer if he fell on them," Barry said. I was embarrassed for him. I looked away, not wanting to make eye contact with him.

The bar continued to fill up with passengers until it was crowded. Through the window, we could see the police running past outside. My friends and I huddled together. I noticed that Pat was drinking something pink in a martini glass.

"What is that? Another of their lethal specials?" I asked her.

"It's a Shirley Temple," Pat said, smiling. "I decided to lay off for a while. A Shirley Temple seemed really appropriate."

"Good for you, Pat," I said. "We could probably all drink less."

I put down my Desperatador, waved to the

waitress, and pointed to Pat's drink and then to myself.

"How did you have the presence of mind to spray Lysol at him?" Mary Louise asked. "I would have been paralyzed. What if he hadn't missed when he shot at you?"

"You'd be surprised at what you can do when someone is pointing a gun at you," I said. "It's like every cell in your brain concentrates on surviving. It still hasn't hit me yet. I'll probably fall apart later."

"Is there any Lysol left?" Mary Louise asked teasingly. "I want to spray every surface that creep touched."

"I'll buy you a new can," I said. "And I promise, I'll never call you a germ freak again."

An hour later, the inspector's voice came over the loudspeaker again.

"Ladies and gentlemen, your attention please. We have searched the ship. The assailant is not on it. We think he was able to slip ashore on one of the supply boats and we are transferring our search to St. Petersburg. You are free to leave the Skylight Bar and return to your regular activities. Unfortunately, you will not be able to tour St. Petersburg today, but we hope that will change tomorrow. Your cruise director has asked me to announce that dinner will be served tonight, though it may be a more informal meal than you are used to."

"I'm not sure I believe that everything is all right," Alex said. "I'm not convinced that the murderer got off this ship. How could he, with everyone looking for him? I'm going to stay here and try to find out more." He put his arm around Gini. "And I want to be sure all of you are all right. We can't have anything happen to our favorite entertainers."

Gini looked relieved. "I'm so glad you're staying," she said.

"Oh, Alex," I said, starting to shake again. "Do you really think he's still on this ship? I don't want to run into the man with the gun again. I'm all out of Lysol."

"I'm sorry, Tina," Alex said. "I shouldn't have said that. If the police say he's not on board then he isn't on board. Anyway, we're not letting you out of our sight. Are you actually going to dance tonight after what you've been through?"

"I don't know if Heidi wants us to dance tonight," I said. "I'll see what she says. And then I'll see if my feet will obey my brain."

People were milling about trying to decide what to do, where to go.

"Ms. Powell, Ms. Powell," said the familiar voice of Heidi. Since learning about her transgendered past, I now saw her as a strong and serious presence. I thought she was incredibly brave to do what she did. I can't even begin to imagine how painful her life must have been before she changed from a man into a woman. But did she kill Allgood to keep people from knowing about it?

"Ms. Powell," she said, "I don't know how to ask you this." She stopped, uncertain whether to continue or not.

"It's OK, Heidi," I said, knowing what she was reluctant to ask. "I'll be all right by tonight. Don't worry. I think I'll be able to dance. In fact, it might help. Dancing always helps."

She looked relieved.

"Are you sure?" she asked. "You haf been through a terrible experience, so I vould understand if you didn't feel up to it. I could ask the captain to give his little talk about channels and weather conditions and how the locks in the river work."

My friends and I looked at each other. Locks in the river? The weather? We shook our heads.

"I'm all right, Heidi," I said. "We'll dust off our tap shoes and knock their socks off."

"That vould be gut."

"Heidi," I said, "will Sergei be cooking for us again tonight?"

"Yes, he will be the chef for the rest of the cruise. Everyone was pleased with the meal he prepared last night."

"It was fantastic," I said. "He's a truly talented cook."

I gathered my group around me and told them we'd be dancing that night. "I think we should travel in packs," I said. "Alex is worried that the murderer might still be on this ship, and I'd just as soon not run into him again."

Tina's Travel Tip: There probably won't be a murder on your cruise, so follow Caroline's ten rules of life and have fun.

Chapter 16

Happy Birthday, Caroline!

"Where's Janice?" I asked when we sat down at our table for dinner.

"She was still in our cabin when I left," Pat said. "She was talking on her cell."

"Who was she talking to?" I asked.

"I don't know. She went in the bathroom and closed the door. I couldn't hear her end of the conversation."

"Hope everything is all right at home," Mary Louise said as she studied the evening's menu. "Look—beef stroganoff tonight. Let's see what Sergei can do with that."

I motioned to Olga, who came over to our table. "Olga, is the beef stroganoff good?"

"Potatoes or green beans?" she said.

"Beans," I said, giving up.

In a few minutes, Olga appeared with our dinners.

"Mmmmm," Gini said after her first bite. "This is perfection. Beautifully cooked beef in some kind of lovely cream sauce. Wait till you taste it."

"I've got to get this recipe," Mary Louise said. "I make stroganoff at home but it doesn't taste like this."

Janice came running up to the table. She was smiling.

"Guess what?" she said. "Oh, I can't wait to tell you."

"What is it, Jan?" I asked, eager to hear her news.

"My daughter, Sandy, called me," she said. "It's the first time in two years we've talked to each other."

"Oh, Janice, that's wonderful," Pat said. "Why did she call?"

"It's so exciting. She's writing a book about the Gypsy Robes, and she wants me to work on it with her. I can't believe it!"

"What are Gypsy Robes?" Mary Louise said.

"It's a tradition in the theater," Janice said. "At the opening of every new musical in New York, a robe is passed on to the dancer—they call the chorus line dancers *gypsies*—who has danced in the most musicals on Broadway. The robe is covered with souvenirs from other shows—like parts

179

of costumes or playbills or photos of other dancers. Half an hour before the show opens, the winner circles the whole group while each gypsy reaches out and touches the robe for good luck. There are about fourteen of them now and some of them are in the Smithsonian in Washington. One of my friends is the official historian of the Gypsy Robes. She has photographs and all kinds of information. Sandy and I are going to produce the book together. Can't you just imagine how beautiful it will be—the colors, the costumes, the history?"

"Sounds wonderful," Pat said. "But the best part is you'll be working with Sandy. Is everything OK between you two now?"

"It's a start," Janice said. "We have a lot to talk about before everything is really all right. But we'll get there. I was so young when I had her. I made a lot of mistakes while I was bringing her up. Hearing her voice was like getting a hug from her."

"If I can help . . . ," Pat said.

"I'd love your help," she said, smiling at her friend.

"Ms. Temple," Heidi said. "Here is recipe. Sergei said is not hard to make. You can watch him next time."

"Heidi, you're the best. Very . . . uh . . . *gut*," Mary Louise said.

Stacy and Andrea burst into our conversation,

both of them full of energy and enthusiasm. "Hey Hoofers, you're invited to a birthday party," Stacy said.

"You have to come over to our table," Andrea said. "We're cutting Nana's birthday cake. She asked especially that you five join us. Please, please say you'll come."

"I wouldn't miss your grandmother's birthday party for anything," I said. My friends were out of their chairs and on their way to Caroline's table before I got the words out of my mouth.

"Happy birthday, Caroline," I said, giving her a hug. "You look beautiful."

She was wearing a light blue silk dress that made her eyes look even bluer. Sapphire blue earrings against her white hair gave her whole face a vivid, lively beauty that we all envied.

"I want to look just like you when I'm eighty," Janice said.

"Don't wish your life away," Caroline said. "Take your time getting here. But, thank you."

Two of the waitresses brought a large white cake with pink and blue buttercream roses. Written on the top in icing was *Rock on Nana!* It was topped by eight candles.

"I love you two hooligans," she said to her granddaughters, and paused to make a wish before blowing out the candles.

"What did you wish for, Caroline?" Mary Louise asked.

"I wished that all of you would have half the fun I've had in my life and that you all end up with people to love," she said, looking at her two granddaughters, her eyes bright with tears.

Stacy and Andrea kissed their grandmother and cut pieces of cake for all of us. As we gobbled up Sergei's divine devil's food cake, Stacy said, "We have a surprise for you, Nana."

"What terrible thing have you done now?" she asked.

"Andy and I made up a song about your ten rules of life you're always telling us about."

We all cheered.

"Let's hear it," Caroline said, obviously delighted that her granddaughters had gone to all this trouble for her.

Andrea and Stacy stood up, did a little dance, turned around, and sang to their grandmother:

> *Never whine about your aches and pains*
> *Or moan and groan whenever it rains.*
> *Tap dance instead—you'll make people smile*
> *Try everything once—you'll find it*
> *   worthwhile.*
> *Always be sure you have money of your own,*
> *And always say I love you before you hang up*
> *   the phone.*
> *Make lots of friends—they're better than gold,*
> *Forgive your parents—they can't help being*
> *   old.*

Make people you meet feel glad they're alive
Get rid of the grouches—they barely survive.
And finally most important of all—
Love one another—and just have a ball!

The girls gave one last high kick and grapevined over to their grandmother. We all cheered and applauded as they gave her a hug and a kiss. Other passengers stood up and clapped too, obviously delighted at the girls' performance.

"Those are perfect rules of life, Caroline," Pat said. "No wonder you look the way you do at eighty."

"You girls are doing all the right things," she said. "I wish I could be around to come to your eightieth birthday parties, but I'll be up there watching you and sending you my love."

We were quiet, absorbing Caroline's wisdom, picturing ourselves at eighty. I thought about the things that were most meaningful to me—my daughters, my friends, my memories of Bill—and Peter popped into my mind. I had a sudden urge to call him.

"Thank you, Caroline, for letting us be a part of your birthday party," I said. "We'll never forget you or your granddaughters. And now, if you'll excuse us, we Hoofers have to change for our performance tonight."

Pat joined me, and we walked downstairs together.

"Are you sure you can do this, Tina?" Pat asked. "I don't know how you can even walk, much less dance, after what happened."

"I'm tougher now, Pat."

When we got to our cabins, I called Peter while Gini was taking a shower. The phone rang . . . and rang . . . until Peter's recorded voice said, "This is Peter Simpson. I'm sorry to miss your call. Please leave a message and I'll get back to you soon."

Where could he be? And who could he be with? A wave of homesickness washed over me, and suddenly I missed him terribly.

I left a message: "It's Tina. Things are a little crazy here, but I'm fine. How are you? Call me."

I showered after Gini was through, and we changed into our red, white, and blue sparkly outfits of short shorts, jackets, and Uncle Sam top hats, with black sequined stockings and red tap shoes. "Let's start out with 'Yankee Doodle Dandy,' then 'You're a Grand Old Flag,' and end with 'I Got Rhythm,' " I said.

"Maybe we should put 'I Got Rhythm' in the middle and end with a rousing 'Grand Old Flag,' " Pat said.

"Good idea," I said. "Gini, will you put the CDs in the right order please? We've got a show to put on."

CHORUS LINES, CAVIAR, AND CORPSES

* * *

We bounced onto the stage that night looking like the American flag in motion, and worked the march step and the high kicks and the salutes for all they were worth. The audience was cheering and clapping and singing along with us. It was as if the horror of the day had been conquered by five tap-dancing American women in the prime of their lives, giving their all for their country, with happy endings and great legs. By the time we ended with "You're a Grand Old Flag," the old man in the front row was standing with his hand over his heart while Old Glory waved in back of us, blown by the rickety fan Heidi had dug up in some storeroom.

At the end, Tatiana rushed up to us and gave us all hugs. "Today, I feel like an American," she said. "Where do I sign up?" Even the Russian crew was smiling and cheering us on. Sergei gave us the thumbs up sign.

We celebrated on deck, reveling in the light-filled White Night, which lasted until the sun came up around three in the morning. The Russians call this phenomenon *Belye Nochi*. The White Nights start in late May and continue until mid-July, during which time there are festivals, concerts, and art shows in St. Petersburg which continue until dawn. We let the rush of adrenaline always generated by a performance subside before going off to bed and instant sleep.

Tina's Travel Tip: Don't miss the chance to watch the chef prepare something delicious in the kitchen.

Chapter 17

You're the Beef in My Stroganoff

At breakfast the next morning, Sergei came to our table to ask if I was all right.

"Thank you, Sergei," I said. "I'm still a little shaky. I'm worried that the murderer is still somewhere on this ship and I'm scared to death he'll jump out of some closet and get me again."

"Police say he is gone. If police say he's gone, then he's gone," Sergei said. "Is there anything I can do to help you?"

"Well . . . ," I said, hesitating. "I don't mean to steal your secrets, Sergei, but that stroganoff last night was the best I've ever had. Would you mind telling me how you did it?"

"Of course," he said, holding out his hand. "Come to kitchen and I show you recipe."

"Oh, could I watch too?" Mary Louise said.

"You are welcome," Sergei said. "Anyone else?"

"Think I'll just have another cup of coffee, thanks, Sergei," Pat said, taking another sip.

"I'm saving my energy for St. Petersburg," Janice said. "Thanks anyway, Sergei."

Gini still hadn't shown up for breakfast, so Mary Louise and I followed Sergei into the kitchen.

"Look, I show you," he said. "This is beef I use, and it must be best filet mignon. Whole success of stroganoff is quality of beef. Must be excellent."

"But it was the sauce that was outstanding, Sergei," Mary Louise said. "What did you put in there?"

"First you cut the meat into strips, flour it, and brown it—very fast—in butter. Add onions, mushrooms, and garlic, and cook them only until onion is tender. Don't cook too much. Take out of pan and keep warm. More butter in pan and—"

"Good thing our no-butter lady isn't here," Mary Louise said.

"Sometimes you must have butter. Nothing else tastes as good," Sergei said.

"How do you stay so thin when you eat all this butter and cream and stuff?" I asked.

"I am always moving, walking, biking, always doing something that gets rid of fat when I'm not cooking. Also, I don't eat so much. No time."

"No wonder you look so fit. Anyway, what comes next? Add more butter to pan and . . ."

"Then blend in flour, add tomato paste, and slowly pour in beef stock if you have it, beef broth if not. Keep stirring with a whisk until it looks thick. Put meat and mushrooms back in sauce, put in sour cream and sherry, and you have stroganoff."

"I do all that when I make my stroganoff," Mary Louise said, "but it just doesn't come out like yours. What am I doing wrong?"

"Remember, beef must be the very, very best. And I think we do get better mushrooms here than you do. All our vegetables are fresher, I think."

"So I have to shop here in Russia before I make any of the dishes you showed us how to make?"

Sergei laughed. "Just come here to live and you will make great food every time."

"Thanks, Sergei," I said. "You're so nice to take all this time with us."

"You are Happy Hoofers," he said. "Trip better because of you."

We thanked him and went back to the dining room. Gini and Alex were there now, talking animatedly, when we sat down again at our table.

"What's happening?" I asked Alex. "Anything new?"

Alex stopped talking and looked at me with a worried expression. "Well, there is something new, but I don't want to ruin your day, Tina."

"Oh no. Now what? The killer is hiding in my closet or something?"

"No, it's just that . . ." He looked at Gini, as if asking her if he should go on.

"What? You can tell me," I said, not at all sure I wanted to hear.

"They found some food missing from the kitchen—Sergei keeps careful track of every item that goes in or out of the pantry. It could just be one of the other cooks or dishwashers or waitresses who took it, but the police are afraid whoever killed the chef and Sasha is hiding somewhere on the ship. They're going to search every inch of the ship again while we're in St. Petersburg today. Don't worry, Tina, they'll make sure he isn't here."

"That's what they said before," I said, really scared now. "*Oh don't worry,* they said, *we're sure the murderer is not on the ship.* Yet somehow he manages to hide somewhere."

"Look," Alex said, "come see St. Petersburg. It's so beautiful, you'll forget all about yesterday's incident. And we're not going to leave you alone, ever. You're safe."

MARY LOUISE'S RECIPE FOR BEEF STROGANOFF

¼ cup flour
½ teaspoon salt
1 pound filet mignon or sirloin, cut in strips
¼ cup butter
1¼ cups sliced mushrooms
½ cup chopped onions
2 cloves minced garlic
¼ teaspoon nutmeg
1 tablespoon tomato paste
12 ounces beef broth
1 cup sour cream
3 tablespoons sherry

1. Salt the meat and dredge it in 1 tablespoon of the flour.
2. Brown beef in half the butter and add mushrooms, onion, garlic, and nutmeg. Cook until onions are wilted.
3. Transfer meat and mushrooms to a warmed plate. Add the rest of the butter to the pan and blend in the rest of the flour. Add the tomato paste and slowly pour in the beef stock. Stir until thick.
4. Put the meat and mushrooms back in the pan. Add the sour cream and sherry and heat

until warm. Serve with noodles and a green salad.

Serves two.

Spasiba, Sergei! (You already know this means "thank you," Sergei!)

Chapter 18

Now You See It, Now You Don't

I followed everybody out to the bus where Andrei was waiting for us. Still his usual indifferent self, he tried to look as if he was glad to see us. He managed to dredge up a half smile and ushered us onto the bus. He still wore a shirt and tie, but his red vest had been replaced by a dark blue gabardine jacket.

Barry called to me as we took our seats.

"I saved this seat for you, Tina."

"Oh, that's OK, Barry. I need to talk to my fellow dancers about our routine." I gave him a small smile as I passed by.

He caught my hand. "I'll catch up with you in the museum," he said.

Andrei told us about The Hermitage as we drove through the streets of St. Petersburg, past tall white office buildings and domed cathedrals, which were often on the banks of one of the canals that flowed throughout the city. We could have been driving along the Seine in Paris, the city was so beautifully planned and built. The people walking along the sidewalks on their way to work were dressed as if they were in New York. No long dresses and aprons, no flowered scarves around their heads, just tailored suits and modest dresses, cardigan sweaters over neat slim pants. Sensible shoes or boots. I pressed my face against the window to see every building, bridge, and elegant shop I could spot.

"We will see paintings by da Vinci, Caravaggio, Titian, great masters," Andrei said, and I turned around in my seat to listen to him. "You must stay near me because are big crowds this week. Is school holiday and the museums are packed with Russian families as well as tourists. If you lose me, we meet in the lobby of the museum. I show you when we go in." He waved his numbered sign. "Look for number twenty. Best paintings are on main floor where I take you. If you wish, you can go up to third floor to see third-rate paintings by Impressionists—Renoir, Gauguin, Degas—all those so-called artists who are not so good."

I almost jumped out of my seat in protest. Impressionist painters are my favorites. A print of Renoir's *A Girl with a Watering Can* is hanging in my bedroom at home. I always head straight for the sun-filled rooms in museums with Impressionist paintings in them. I love the light, the soft colors, the flowers, the rounded pink nudes, the rosy cheeked children, and the tutu-wearing dancers. Evidently, this is all too decadent for Andrei.

The bus stopped and there it was—the Hermitage. The museum I've wanted to see all my life. We climbed out of the coach and stood in Palace Square. We stared at the blue and white Winter Palace of the tsars, who lived there until 1917, when the Communist revolutionaries killed all the royals. I was awed by the size of it. Six buildings stretching along one side of the square held three million art exhibits. All were painted light blue and white, with two floors of windows side by side stretching the whole width of the palace. If you stayed there a week, looking at paintings and sculpture all day long, you'd never see all of it.

The path leading up to the museum was filled with people, children and adults, black and white, Russians and tourists, hurrying toward the doors. Andrei led our little group into the museum and then up a long flight of white marble steps with a red carpet running up the center. With each step, my excitement grew.

"It's the biggest art museum in the world," I heard Alex say to Gini. "Way bigger than the Metropolitan in New York, and ornate in the way only the Russian tsars—and French kings— could manage. You'll see gold and marble columns and ceilings covered with paintings and carvings, enormous crystal chandeliers dwarfed by the size of the rooms they hang in."

"Follow me. Stay close," Andrei said as we struggled to keep up with him. Barry tried to push his way through to walk with me, but my friends formed a tight circle around me so he couldn't get through.

We walked into the Italian Renaissance room. Each group was allowed only a limited amount of time to go through the main part of the museum. Hundreds of school children, foreign tourists, and Russian families rushed from painting to painting. We stared, overwhelmed at the extravagantly ornate gold and crystal chandeliers, highly polished parquet floors, domed cathedral ceilings. Oddly, the paintings themselves were hung in a hodgepodge way in bad lighting, so it was very hard to see them.

"Hurry, hurry," Andrei said. "Here is Leonardo." We each had about one minute to look at a small daVinci on an easel in the middle of the room. It was an oil painting of the *Madonna and Child*, beautiful and serene, but hardly in the right place to show off its perfection.

"Do not stay too long with each picture," Andrei said. "Next, we see Caravaggio over here." He herded us over to a painting hung on the wall, but the light coming in from the window cast a glare on the glass covering the work of art, so it was hard to make out the subject of the painting. It was Caravaggio's *Lute Player,* which I knew showed a young boy in a white shirt against a dark background. Squinting, I could barely make out the central figure.

We heard angry voices and without even turning around, I knew Barry was at the center of the disturbance. He refused to leave the *Madonna and Child,* and the guide of another tourist group was trying to get him to move along.

"I have not finished looking at this painting," Barry shouted. "I will leave when I'm good and ready."

Andrei rolled his eyes and hurried over to Barry. He said something in Russian to the other guide. To Barry, he said, "Please, Mr. Martin, I want you to see a magnificent Rubens across the room." Barry made grumbling noises, but followed Andrei to a painting called *Statue of Ceres,* which showed the earth goddess with little cherubs carrying fruits and vegetables to place around her statue.

Seconds later, Andrei scooted us to another part of the main floor. "This museum has largest collection of Rembrandts," he said. We caught a glimpse of *Return of the Prodigal Son* before he shooed us along to a gorgeous Tiepolo.

"This is an outrage," Barry said. "We're going too fast to see anything."

"I am sorry," Andrei said, "but is very busy time of year. You should come back in the wintertime. Hardly anyone here. You can see all pictures much better."

"I'm never coming back to this backward country—winter, spring, summer, or fall!" Barry said.

We all cringed. How could I ever have thought this man was interesting or worth knowing? I would have to figure out a way to get rid of him once and for all. Short of pushing him in front of the bus, I didn't know how to do it. I should have known I could count on Gini.

"Barry, Andrei is doing the best he can," she said. "I suggest you take your anger and stuff it. In any case, stay away from us. We've had enough of you."

Barry looked at me.

"And that includes our friend Tina here," Gini said. Her expression was easy to read. "Leave her alone."

I nodded. He got the message.

Andrei, looking relieved, waved for all of us to come over to him. "We still have half an hour before we leave for tour of St. Petersburg," he said.

"If you want, you can go up to third floor and see Impressionists. Not very good, but go if you like. I wait for you here. Meet me by these benches."

Most of us ran up the stairway to the third floor. I found a remarkable collection of works by my favorite painters, many of which I had never seen before, even in art books. There was Renoir's *Girl with a Fan,* a lovely light and pastel-colored painting of an alluring young lady. We saw Matisse's *The Dance,* a vivid abstract painting of five bright-red nudes in a circle, holding hands and dancing so wildly you could almost see them moving. There were paintings by Gauguin and Degas, Van Gogh and Picasso. It wasn't very crowded up there, I guess because the paintings are not respected in this country—at least if we could judge by Andrei's attitude toward them.

"These are my favorites," I said to Pat.

"Mine too," she said. "When we get back home, I'm spending a whole day at the Metropolitan, mostly in the Impressionist part. I never get tired of them. I'm so glad you're writing about this trip, Tina. It's been a fascinating experience—well, except for a murder here and there, but I wouldn't have missed it for anything."

"I'm relieved that you feel that way, Pat," I said. "I was afraid I'd led all of us into something really dangerous for a while there. But we're safe now—or at least I think we are—and we can enjoy our last day of the cruise."

"I hope you're right, Tina. I'm a little worried that guy will turn up again on the ship." She saw the look on my face and quickly added, "Oh, Tina, I didn't mean that. I'm sure he left the ship. Don't worry. Please forget I said that."

"I still get the shakes when I think about him," I said. "But I'm telling myself the police searched the ship thoroughly, and they would have found him by now if he were still on the ship. Right?"

"Of course," Pat said, putting her arm around me. "He's gone. You'll never see him again."

I knew she was just trying to make me feel better, but I was grateful for her fake reassurance.

We walked back to the lobby of the Hermitage to join Alex, who brightened up the minute he saw Gini.

"This is no way to see the Hermitage," he said to her. "I wish I could show it to you without all these people. If you were going to be here longer, I might be able to arrange a private showing, but this is your last day." He looked at Gini and we could tell that he wanted her to stay as long as he was posted in Moscow.

"I'll be back," Gini said. "I'd love to do a documentary on St. Petersburg. It's full of possibilities."

"There's so much I could show you," Alex said.

Mark and Sue walked over to join us. They looked a little down in the mouth, not their usual enthusiastic selves.

"Somehow, this isn't what I expected visiting the Hermitage would be like," Sue said. "I could have spent hours just looking at the Rembrandts."

"My bride was really looking forward to this part of the trip," Mark said.

"We're all disappointed, Mark," Pat said. "We just came at the wrong time of year, that's all."

"What do you paint, Sue?" I asked.

"Mostly still lifes and landscapes. We live in Colorado, and our house faces the mountains. Mark built me my own studio. It's really beautiful. You have to come and visit us."

"I'd love to," I said. "I've always wanted to see Colorado."

Caroline came up beside us in a wheelchair being pushed by her granddaughters.

"Caroline, are you all right?" I said.

"Oh yes, dear, I'm fine. Andrei offered to get me a wheelchair because of the crowds. The girls and I decided it would be a good idea. I'm glad I said yes. A person could get trampled here."

"It's a good thing Andrei thought of that," I said. "It's rough going through these crowds."

I was glad to see that Stacy and Andrea were making sure their grandmother saw everything, while being protected from the shoving and pushing all around us.

"Are you going to the ballet tonight?" I asked them. "To see *Nutcracker*?"

"Oh yes," Stacy said with a spark of mischief in her eyes. "Andy and I are going to sneak in and join the dancers under the Christmas tree. No one would notice a couple more kids, and we'll scrunch down."

"I'm afraid I've been a very bad influence on you," I said, laughing at these wonderful girls. "But that does sound like fun."

"Don't encourage them," Caroline said. "They really would do it."

We formed a protective circle around Caroline and her wheelchair until we found Andrei again near the benches. He led us to the square in front of the museum, where our coach was waiting for us.

"Oh, Tina," Pat said, "look at all those cats running around. There are so many of them."

"They're a tradition at the Hermitage," a woman wearing glasses and a sensible dark blue suit, one of our fellow passengers, said to us as we headed for the bus.

"What do you mean?" Pat asked.

"When Empress Elizabeth started collecting paintings for the palace, she wanted to protect them from mice and rats. She brought in a bunch of cats to catch them, and they still do that."

"I didn't see any in the museum," I said.

"They're not allowed in the galleries, but there are about sixty-five of them. They live in the basement and run around out here in the square."

"How do you know all this?" Pat asked her.

"I love cats and I read about them in a guide-book before I came here."

Pat leaned over to pet a black and white cat, who rubbed against her leg.

"They certainly look healthy," she said.

"They should," the woman said. "There are three people who are hired to take care of them and make sure they have food and medical care."

"What a great country," Pat said.

"Please to take your seat on bus," Andrei said. "We will do city tour so you will view the great beauty of St. Petersburg." Andrei actually sounded enthusiastic, for once. We piled back on the coach and plunked down in our seats.

As the driver eased his way out of the crowded plaza, Andrei picked up his microphone again. "Peter the Great called this city his Window to the West," he said. "He wanted it to be like other European cities—like Paris—reflecting Western culture, because so much of Russia had been under the influence of Eastern cultures before he became tsar. This city has sixty-six canals, a hundred and one islands, and hundreds of bridges. You feel like you are in Europe. You will find box lunches on your seats for you to eat on our way to Catherine Palace."

Tina's Travel Tip: Don't worry about the extra calories you eat on a cruise. You'll walk them off sightseeing. Yeah, right.

Chapter 19

The St. Petersburg Diet

As the bus moved along the crowded streets, occasionally dodging horse-drawn carriages, we opened our box lunches to find ham sandwiches, an apple, and a cookie. "So Russian," Mary Louise murmured.

"One thing about this trip," Gini said, "we won't gain any weight. It may be the first cruise in history where you come back thinner than when you left."

"See," I said, "there's always a silver lining. I've been on every diet known to womankind, and I had to go on a cruise to lose weight."

Pat leaned over the back of her seat as the bus pulled out into traffic. "What diets have you been on? I thought you were just naturally thin, Tina."

"Naturally thin is sixteen years old," Mary Louise said. "Ever-expanding hips and stomachs and waistlines are from thirty-five on. If George didn't keep nagging me about staying skinny, I'd be nicely rounded."

"Honestly," Janice said, "I don't know why you put up with that bully. Why do you let him tell you what you can and can't do? You're fifty-two years old and you act like his slave."

"I've been married for thirty years, Jan, and I'd like to stay that way for another thirty," Mary Louise said, uncharacteristically snappish. "Not everyone changes husbands as often as her underwear."

"My husbands were no prizes," Janice said. "But they never tried to tell me what to do or not do. You're such a wimp. I'll bet you had to cook all week before you left so there would be dinners in the freezer for George, assuming he even knows where the freezer is."

"Well, what if I did? I love him and I want him to eat well while I'm away. Sometimes marriage is eighty-twenty. Too bad you never learned that. We don't all have a steel rod up our kazoos."

"With you, you're always the eighty and he's always the twenty," Janice said.

"Enough," Pat said, her therapist voice taking over. "Why don't you stop George-bashing, Janice. And Mary Louise, stop defending your marriage all the time. It is what it is and you obviously like it that way. So knock it off, both of you."

Janice and Mary Louise glowered at each other.

"I'll shut up about George if you shut up about my three marriages," Janice said.

Mary Louise put out her hand to shake on the deal. "It's a good thing Pat is here," she said.

"We're all glad Pat is here," I said. "But let's get back to diets. Wanna hear how I lost twelve pounds on my chocolate and wine diet?"

A slightly plump woman with a shiny face, who was wearing a blouse not tucked into her pants, leaned in closer. "That's my kind of diet. You just eat chocolate and drink wine all day?"

"Not really," I said. "But I knew I would never stick to any diet that didn't include a glass of wine at dinner and a little chocolate. So I allowed myself a glass of wine or two and nibbled on these fabulous rich, dark chocolate cookies I found that have only twenty calories each."

"But how did you lose the twelve pounds?" practical Pat asked. "What did you eat in between the wine and the chocolate?"

"I made up a twelve-hundred calorie a day diet that had lots of fruits and veggies, some chicken and fish, nuts for snacks, and I exercised. Mostly danced."

"I'm starting that diet the minute I get home," the plump lady said.

"It certainly beats that low-fat, no-fat, whole grain boring stuff we eat all the time," Mark said from his seat behind us. "I know it's good for me, and Sue is just trying to keep me around to entertain her. But once in a while, I'd like a nice fattening Danish for breakfast."

Sue patted his stomach. "You're much more entertaining without a fat belly."

Mark put his arm around her. "I knew I was just your plaything."

"I think Andrei is trying to get our attention," Pat said.

Our guide picked up his microphone as the bus neared a massive structure of wood and stone. "The crowning glory of Tsar Peter's reign was the Peter and Paul Fortress, built in the eighteenth century. Inside this fortress is the Peter and Paul Cathedral, where Peter is buried and also the Romanovs, the last tsars before the Communist Revolution in 1917," he said.

The bus stopped briefly so we could look at St. Isaac's Cathedral, which Andrei told us was the largest in the city, with more than 200 pounds of gold in the dome. "It holds thirteen thousand people . . . ," he was saying when I fell asleep.

I woke up an hour later, stretched, and asked Mary Louise if I had missed anything.

"Only about a thousand monuments, statues, churches, canals, and bridges," she said. "But you woke up in time for Catherine Palace."

Catherine the Great's summer palace was a

blue and white confection of glistening marble and gold statues, with fountains shooting water into the air all along the length of the edifice. "Longest palace in world," Andrei said. He led us into the Great Hall, a glittering glass and gold ballroom lined with two tiers of mirrors and windows.

"Look at that ceiling," Gini said. A vast painting of Russian victories and figures representing art and science stretched above us across the whole room, which made the football stadium in my hometown seem small by comparison.

"What do you think, Sue?" I asked her. "Your kind of painting?"

"Mine tend to be a little smaller," she said, smiling. "But I love this room. Just look at all the light and sparkle and gold. It feels much more European than Russian. Doesn't it remind you of the Hall of Mirrors in Versailles?"

"I was just thinking that," I said, turning around to take in the elaborate décor of the palace. "You and Mark must have been to Paris many times."

"Yes, in fact I lived there when I was eighteen," she said. "I studied painting there."

"Oh, Sue, I lived there too," Gini said. "After I graduated from college, I studied photography in Paris. It's still my favorite place in the world." She pulled Sue off to the side, and I could tell from their gestures and mouth pursings they were talking in French.

"This palace is in town now called Pushkin,

after great Russian poet," Andrei said. It was obvious he was delighted at this change.

We walked through the ornate rooms, feasting our eyes on the elegant furniture, the marble and silk wall coverings, the huge blue and white tiled ovens that kept Catherine and her minions warm. The sweet sound of a string quartet playing in one of the chandeliered halls followed us as we moved from room to room.

Andrei led us outside to the back of the palace, past a large pyramid structure. "Catherine's dogs buried here," he said. We crossed a marble bridge over what was called "the Great Pond" and checked out the pavilion where musicians had played for the tsars and their guests.

"During White Nights, we have chamber music concerts here at the palace," Andrei said. "Beautiful."

Sated with the glories of the days of Russia's tsars, we piled back onto the bus and headed back to the ship.

Tina's Travel Tip: If you can't dance, watch someone else do it—preferably the Bolshoi Ballet.

Chapter 20

Sugar Plum Fairies and Snowflakes

For our dinner that night, Sergei had prepared an exemplary chicken Kiev that even Alex approved of. He and Gini were talking earnestly to each other at the other end of the table. I couldn't hear what they were saying, but I did hear New York mentioned several times.

"This is really good Kiev," Mary Louise said. "I wish I could take Sergei back home with me to cook for George. Maybe he wouldn't complain so much about my dinners."

"You're a fantastic cook," I said. "George should be grateful to have you cooking for him."

"Well, it's just that he's very fussy about food," she said. "When we got married, I wanted to make great meals for him every night. I cooked all these complicated recipes by Julia Child and Jacques Pépin and Lidia what's-her-name—the Italian chef. Lidia Bastianich. We would have beef bourguignon one night, veal marengo the next, venison, duck confit, rabbit. It would take me hours to make dinner—all that chopping and simmering and burning myself. Sometimes I just got sick of it—you know?"

"Didn't you ever hear of Chinese takeout or pizza delivery?" Janice said.

"Of course," Mary Louise said. "But George wouldn't eat any of that stuff. It was either my cooking or some good restaurant. It's my own fault—I spoiled him."

"You think?" Janice said.

"Well, he's still there, unlike—"

Heidi rang a little bell and stood to make her farewell speech. She looked majestic in her crisp white shirt and tailored blue uniform, her hair twisted into an elaborate braid.

"Saved by the bell," I said to Janice.

"Ve hope that you have not been put off our Russian river cruises by a little murder or two," Heidi said, and there was some nervous laughter. Our serious-minded Heidi had actually made a joke—possibly the first in her life. To tell you the truth, I didn't think it was all that funny.

"Inspector Gregarin assures me that his detectives have searched the ship from bottom to top, looked in every closet and possible hiding place. The man who murdered Chef Allgood is positively, definitely not on this ship. You can relax. Most of the time, everyone comes back home alive from our cruise, and the food is excellent. Next trip, I make sure Sergei cooks for us from the beginning of the cruise." We all cheered and Sergei appeared from the kitchen, smiling and blushing.

"For those of you who are still alive—oh, I mean still *awake*," Heidi said—her second joke!—and we all groaned, "ve vill take you to the theater tonight to see our famous Bolshoi dancers. They dance Tchaikovsky's *Nutcracker Suite.* It is very very beautiful and if you can possibly go, you should.

"I vant to thank especially the Happy Hoofers, who not only danced their tootsies off for us"—here Heidi smiled modestly at having mastered another English idiom before continuing—"but Tina Powell risked her life while she was on board. Here's to the Happy Hoofers, with the wish that they will come back and dance for us again."

"The day after never," Gini muttered.

We got a standing ovation.

"And now, I have a special surprise for all of you. Because of the unfortunate occurrences on our cruise, you could not get off the ship and see some of the sights that were included on your trip. Ve are prepared to make that up to you. If you vish, you may stay on the ship as we sail back to Moscow. You may accompany Andrei on a tour of the city, see our fabulous circus, with tigers and bears and trapeze artists. Ve vill get you to your plane the next day. Ve vill take care of changing your flight reservations."

There was scattered applause. We looked at each other. Did we really want two more days on this cartoon cruise ship with inept service, two murders, one disappearance and bad memories?

"What do you say, Hoofers?" I asked. "Do we stay or go?"

Gini looked at Alex. "I vote to stay," she said.

"I don't know," Janice said. "I think I've had enough. I want to get back to New York to see my daughter."

"Oh, come on, Janice, it's only a couple of days," Mary Louise said. "Just think, we'll get to see Moscow—and the circus. You don't want to miss the Kremlin, do you? Or the dancing bears?"

"When will we get the chance to come back?" Pat asked.

"Never!" I said. "At least, I hope not. I think we should stay. Janice, what do you say? It won't be as much fun without you—but we do understand if you want to get back to see Sandy."

Janice knew we really wanted her to stay. "It does seem too bad to come all this way and not see Moscow," she said. "And I'll be with Sandy in three days. OK, I'm in too."

We all cheered.

"Are we going to the ballet?" I asked. "We don't have to dance tonight, so we might as well watch someone else perform. Want to go?"

In a nanosecond, Janice said, "We have to. When will we ever get the chance to see the Bolshoi dancers in Russia again? Come on, gang."

As usual, when Janice turns on her powers of persuasion, we couldn't turn down this great opportunity.

Sergei brought us our dessert, a chocolate soufflé, and we told him how great his cooking was.

"When I come to America, Ms. Temple," he said to Mary Louise, "you will invite me to dinner? I want to see how you cook my recipes."

"You have to come, Sergei." She reached into her bag and pulled out her card. "This is my address and phone number and e-mail and everything else. I would love to cook for you."

"And this is my last gift to you," Sergei said, handing her a piece of paper. "My recipe for chicken Kiev. Not so difficult, this one. *Priyatnogo appetita.*" He kissed Mary Louise's hand before going back into the kitchen.

As the tour bus drove us through the still-sunlit city to the Bolshoi, I remembered taking my two daughters to see the *Nutcracker* ballet when they were little. They loved it so much, it became a tradition for us to see it every year at Christmastime. Later, Laurie brought her own children to this exquisite ballet and invited me along. I loved to watch their faces as the Christmas tree grew taller and taller until it reached the ceiling during the dream sequence. I was sorry that neither of my daughters had inherited my love of dancing. But there was still hope for my grandchildren.

When the orchestra started to play that familiar music by Tchaikovksy and the heavy burgundy curtain rose on the party at the mansion, I was back at Lincoln Center watching Clara hug her nutcracker doll to her chest after her rotten little brother Fritz grabbed it and broke it and the magical toymaker Uncle Drosselmeyer rescued it and gave it back to her.

In the story, Clara falls asleep under the Christmas tree. In her dream, the tree grows taller and taller, wider and wider, until it fills the back part of the stage. I loved the part where she dreams that her nutcracker doll turns into a handsome prince who dances with her and beautiful snowflake dancers float as light as feathers about the stage.

Best of all was the Sugar Plum Fairy dancing into the scene, all sweetness and light, the music sounding like little bells tinkling around her. The beautiful dancers in white came out to dance the Waltz of the Flowers, their tutus a blossom of turned-up skirts, like the petals of chrysanthemums.

The Spanish dancers clicked and flirted, the Arabian figures turning slowly, their hands pressed together as if in prayer, while Chinese dancers held parasols and embraced Clara. Then, finally, the Russian dancers performed a wonderful sequence, sitting in midair and kicking their legs in a dazzling display of athleticism.

The audience clapped for each group, but the loudest applause was for the Russian dancers. For me, it was a return to my years as a young mother, so long ago now. Where did those years go? Bringing up two little girls was the best part of my life. It seemed impossible that they had grown into incredible women in such a short time. Watching this ballet I loved so much brought it all back so vividly that I felt like I was in the dream with Clara. Looking across the aisle, I saw Caroline, flanked by her teenaged granddaughters, all holding hands like the best of friends. I turned to see Gini, Janice, Mary

Louise, and Pat, my dear friends, and the thought
struck me—families are made, not just born.

At the end, we all clapped and clapped, grateful for this night of beauty and grace, and for
the chance to share it together.

MARY LOUISE'S RECIPE FOR CHICKEN KIEV

6 large boneless, skinless chicken breasts (or more if you're feeding large, hungry men— and I do hope you are!)
2 jumbo eggs
¼ cup water
½ cup flour
3 cups panko
corn oil for deep frying

For the filling:

½ pound softened butter
2 or more tablespoons chopped fresh chives

1. Cream the butter and chives together and chill for about ten minutes or so.
2. Sprinkle the chicken breasts with salt and pepper. Spread the butter and chives mixture over each of the chicken breasts, folding the sides over the mixture to close up. (It should look like a little cigar.) Put in freezer for a few minutes—it's easier to bread them if you do.
3. To bread them, dunk them in the flour first, then in the eggs mixed with the water, and then in the panko, similar to the Cutlets Pojarski.
4. Fill a deep frying pan with the corn oil and heat to 300 degrees, about 3 or 4 inches deep,

and lower the filled chicken breasts into the oil with tongs. Keep turning them until they're cooked through, about 10 minutes or so. Take them out when they're golden brown and cooked.

Serves six.
Horosho!!! That's really good!!!

Chapter 21

Tigers And Jugglers and Bears—Oh My!

When I woke up the next morning, Mary Louise had already taken her shower and was reading.

"Good morning," I said. "I feel great—and I'm starving."

"Me too," she said. "Hurry up and shower and we'll attack the breakfast buffet."

Twenty minutes later, we were in line. The buffet was as scrumptious as ever with meats and cheeses, rolls and breads, jams and butter, cereals and fruit, and your choice of a custom-made omelet or pancakes. Today, something new had been added: the thinnest of crepes filled with creamed chicken and mushrooms that were so light and delicate, you could pretend they had no calories.

Gini and Pat were already at a table eating when we joined them. "This is delicious," Gini said, pouring syrup on her pancakes. "How did you sleep?"

"Like an angel," I said. "Is Janice still asleep?"

"I guess so," Gini said. "I haven't seen her yet."

"I hope she isn't sorry she stayed," I said. "It just wouldn't be the same without her."

"Are you OK, Tina?" Pat asked. "You've been through a lot."

"I'm fine, thanks, Pat. It was a horrible experience, but I feel safe now. The killer must be hiding out somewhere in St. Petersburg. I don't have to worry about meeting him ever again."

"Let's hope you're right," Alex said, joining us.

"Do you know something we don't know, Alex?" Gini asked him.

"Just one small detail that probably doesn't mean anything." He looked around at our faces as we looked up, startled.

"What now?" I asked. "Please don't tell me the murderer could be on this ship."

"Oh, I'm sure he isn't."

"Well, what did you mean—*just one small detail?*"

221

"I saw Sergei this morning after my run," Alex said, looking very uncomfortable. "He told me that some food was missing from the kitchen again. Some bread and fruit—stuff like that. I'm sure one of his workers took it back to his room. Nothing to worry about."

I could not hide the fear in my face.

"Oh. Tina, I'm sorry," he said, patting my arm. "I'm sure it's nothing. Anyway, the police are still on the ship just in case he should turn up. Relax and enjoy Moscow."

I tried to take Alex's advice and relax, without much success.

Janice appeared, her plate full of rolls and cheeses and butter and jams. She had found someone to make her a pot of hot chocolate, so she was totally content.

"Hi, Jan," I said. "Glad you decided to stay?"

"I am," she said. "All it takes is a cup of hot chocolate. Oh, and the best thing just happened."

"What?"

"I just discovered that Mark—Sue's husband—publishes art books. I told him my daughter and I are going to be working on a book about the Gypsy Robes. He thought it sounded like a beautiful book and he wants to talk to me more about it."

"Wouldn't it be great if he published your book?" I said. "Wait until you tell Sandy—she'll be thrilled."

"I know," Janice said, slathering butter on her croissant. "Keep your fingers crossed, Tina."

We walked back to our cabins and gathered cameras and sweaters, as the morning was a little chilly, for our tour of Moscow.

"Good morning, everybody," a cheerful Andrei said when we were seated on the comfortable bus. *Cheerful* was a pleasant surprise coming from our usually unemotional Andrei. "We go now to city of Moscow. We will go to Kremlin Armoury to see the Fabergé eggs and many beautiful things. We cannot go into Red Square because Putin comes tomorrow and it is roped off, but we can look at it. Gum's Department Store is nearby. You must say *Goom*, not Gum, like chewing gum. We go in there. You can shop. Was once office buildings under Stalin. Is now very expensive, decadent mall. You will like."

There were happy murmurs from the women on the bus.

"St. Basil's Cathedral is next to square," Andrei continued. "Supposedly, Ivan the Terrible had the eyes of the architect of this church poked out so he could never make a better one somewhere else. You hear lots of things. Some true. Some not. Then we go for ride on Moscow's subway. Is one hundred and eighty miles long. Carries nine million people every day. Beautiful station stops with statues, paintings. You will like. Afterward, we go to afternoon performance of famous Moscow Circus."

"He had me at Fabergé eggs," Janice whispered.

The bus stopped and Andrei shepherded us into the Kremlin Armoury, the only part of the Kremlin open to the public. Janice had to be dragged away from the display case of porcelain Fabergé eggs, each one sparkling with diamonds, sapphires, pearls, and rubies, with tiny windows showing the delicate carvings inside. "Presents Nicholas the Second and Empress Alexandra gave each other on Easter every year for thirty years," Andrei said, "until they were killed. Artists not paid for these beautiful things. Was totally corrupt society with very rich and very poor."

"Do you get the feeling that communism is not entirely dead here?" Gini said in a low voice to me.

"I know what you mean," I said. "Look at this gold coronation robe. It was Peter the Great's."

"It's amazing the Communists kept all this decadent, monarchist stuff," Gini said.

Andrei heard her. "Is to remind people how rich the tsar was and how poor the people were." He laughed. "Now everybody poor except Russian Mafia."

Andrei took us past royal carriages and elaborate thrones, including a double throne for Peter and his sickly half-brother Ivan. As at the Hermitage, there were tourists everywhere, mostly Russians with their children.

Back outside again, Andrei said, "OK. Rest of Kremlin closed to tourists. But you can see St. Basil's Cathedral—very old—with domes of blue and white and red and gold, all colors very beautiful. Then go to Gum's—best department store in whole world, right over there. Buy what you want. Meet me here in one hour. Then we go on subway."

We looked inside the cathedral. Every inch of the walls and ceiling was covered with paintings. Statues were tucked into every nook and corner. Gold icons of saints dominated the front of the cathedral, and intricate carvings graced the walls and ceilings. Fifteen minutes of this and our eyes needed a rest. "Let's check out Gum's," Mary Louise said, pronouncing it like chewing gum.

"*Goom*, Mary Louise, *Goom*," I said, imitating Andrei.

"Goom, gum, who cares?" she said. "Let's shop."

"You're on," I said. The others decided to check out the buildings surrounding Red Square, so Mary Louise and I headed for the famous department store.

"It's huge," Mary Louise said. And it was. The enormous white building stretched across the east side of Red Square. We walked through the arched entrance into what looked more like a mall than a department store.

The space in Gum's was divided into two sets of shops and boutiques on either side of a wide,

Mary McHugh

tiled pathway, unlike the stores that have one whole floor covered with clothes and shoes and cosmetics counters and stools and bustling crowds pushing their way through the aisles, back at home. On the second and third floors, bridges connected the left side of the store to the right side. The bridge on the top floor was covered with tables with brightly colored umbrellas, where people were eating and drinking.

"This is incredible," Mary Louise said. "Somehow, I wasn't expecting it to be so . . . so . . ."

"Capitalistic?" I said.

"Exactly," she said. "*Vive* Chanel!"

Glittering on either side of us was a series of elegant, very chic boutiques—Chanel, Vuitton, Prada, Armani, Gucci, Versace.

"I was sort of hoping for something more like The Gap," I said, as we walked toward the center of the mall.

In front of the Hugo Boss shop, there was a large blue and white ceramic cow.

"They had these cows in New York a couple of years ago, remember?" I said.

"Right," Mary Louise said, patting the cow's head. "But who'd expect to see them in Moscow in this elegant mall?"

"I never know what to expect in this country," I said, clicking my heels on the tiled floor. "What do you say we tap around this blue and white polka-dot cow?"

"Tina!" Mary Louise said, looking around in alarm. "The KGB, or whatever it's called now, will drag us off to prison."

"I don't think they arrest you for tap dancing," I said, and did a time step around the cow. I couldn't help it. The sound was so great. The clear sound of my heels clicking on this black and white tile was too hard to resist. "Tap your troubles away," I sang, the tiles making my voice sound as if I were in my bathroom at home. Mary Louise couldn't resist. She's like me. Play a little music and we'll follow you anywhere. She started tapping with me and we did our grapevine smoothly around the cow, smiling at the people who stopped to watch us.

"*Amerikanskis*," one old man said to his wife, who frowned. They walked away from us as quickly as possible.

"You're under arrest," a voice behind us said. We turned, startled, and saw Gini, Pat, and Janice watching us from the other side of the cow.

"No disrespectful cow dancing is allowed in Gum's," Janice said.

"That's *Goom's*," Gini said.

We joined arms, threw in a couple of high kicks, and after some more frowns from other shoppers, walked a little more sedately toward the fountain in the middle of the mall. Topping a high column, the fountain spilled water into a pool below, where children threw coins. American pennies and dimes mixed with Russian rubles and others I couldn't identify.

"Did you buy anything?" Janice asked me.

"No," I said. "I didn't see anything authentically Russian. Just stuff I don't buy at home because it's too expensive. But I wouldn't have missed seeing the mall. What time is it, anyway? I think we're supposed to be back at the bus."

"Yeah, it's time," Pat said. "Let's go."

Andrei was waiting for us.

When we were all assembled, he said, "Now we go Ploschad Revolotsii, or Revolution Square. Is only a short distance so we walk there. You will see. Is most beautiful subway system in world.

And it was. We walked down the stairs to the station platform, which looked like the inside of a museum. The floors were so clean, I thought we should take off our shoes.

"Andrei, are those walls marble?" Gini asked, taking out her camera.

"Yes. Stalin wanted these stations to be his legacy," Andrei said. "You will see stained glass decorations here. Chandeliers hang from ceilings that have paintings on them of Russian workers. Different in every station. The columns along each side of the platforms have carving at top."

It was mind-boggling. I found it hard to wrap my brain around the fact that it was a subway station. I'm used to New York's decidedly unfancy platforms. The train roared into the station and Andrei ushered us on board. We sat down on clean seats, admired the spotless floors, and then, startled, I realized there was a dog lying on the floor across from me. Just a dog by himself, alone, without a human being attached.

"Andrei," I said, "how come there's a dog there? He doesn't seem to have an owner."

"Is big problem in subways. No one knows what to do," Andrei said. "About thirty-thousand stray dogs in Moscow who belong to no one. Some of them figured out how to ride subways. They go on specific trains and ride to their stop. People pet them. Give them food. They're all over the city."

"They're not rounded up and put in shelters?" Pat asked.

"No. People say is not dogs' fault they are homeless. Let them alone. But, is problem."

The dog saw me looking at him, got up, and came over.

"He wants food," Andrei said.

I took a cracker out of my bag and held it out to him. He snapped it up and then rubbed against my leg. He was a mutt, sort of a combination Labrador and golden retriever. I could not resist petting him. He looked up at me and his whole body seemed to say, *Take me with you*. Or however you say that in Russian.

I looked over at Pat. "No, Tina," she said, smiling sympathetically. "You can't adopt him. Heidi would not be happy."

The train stopped and Andrei motioned for us to get off. I gave my canine friend one last hug and got off with the others. But the dog followed me off the train. I meant to tell him that he couldn't come with me, but I didn't know how to say it in Russian. He trotted along at my side until we got to the bus, which was waiting for us at the next station. I knelt down beside him and put my arms around him. He put his head on my knee and looked at me with big brown eyes that clearly said, *Please don't send me back out there. I love you.*

"Andrei," I said, "couldn't we take him to the circus with us? They might have some food for him there. And circus people like animals."

"Is no room on bus. I would like to . . . but . . ."

The dog, whom I had named Misha, jumped on the bus and looked back at me, waiting for me to follow him.

"Just to the circus, Andrei. OK?" I said. "He can sit on my feet."

Andrei shrugged. "He's already in bus. But if one of passengers says no, he must go. You understand?"

"Sure," I said. I knew no one could resist this dog.

"Are you nuts?" Gini muttered to me when

she took her seat behind me. "What are you going to do with that dog when it's time to go back to the ship? You can't have a dog there. Think, Tina."

"He wasn't supposed to be on the subway either," I said. "Or on the bus. But guess what?"

Mary Louise slid into the seat beside me. My dog looked up at her, and I know you won't believe me, but he smiled at her. Mary Louise reached over and petted him. "Good dog," she said. "I'll have to ask Elena how to say that in Russian. But, seriously, Tina, you're not really going to keep him, are you?"

She looked at my face. "You *are* going to keep him," she said.

"We'll see," I said.

The other passengers reached over to pet Misha as they passed my seat. He smiled at all of them.

"Under your seats you will find a box lunch to eat while we drive to the theater, where you will see our famous Moscow Circus," Andrei said.

I gave my chicken sandwich to Misha. He made happy dog noises and snuggled closer to me as we pulled up in front of the theater.

Since I didn't know how to say "stay" in Russian, Misha followed me into the theater. Andrei looked in the other direction and pretended not to notice. The lobby was filled with teasers for the show. A couple of acrobats jumped around in one corner, a juggler practiced throwing pins in another, a baby tiger clawed at the bars of his cage, clowns made faces at the children, some of whom started to cry.

"I don't blame them," Gini said. "I was always terrified of clowns when I was a child. I still don't see the point."

"There's no point to clowns," Pat said. "They're just a part of a circus. You sort of expect them."

A little boy came in with his mother, took one look at the clowns, and burst into tears. He clung to his mother and buried his face in her coat. Misha looked at him and then up at me, back to the boy and then up to me again. I knew what he was asking me. I petted him and nodded. "*Da*, Misha," I said, and my kind-hearted dog trotted over to the little boy and nudged him.

The child, who was about five years old, stopped crying, smiled, and reached out to hug Misha. "Mamma," he said, "Danya!"

His mother patted the dog too and looked up to see me watching her.

She must have heard me speaking to my friends, because she spoke to me in English. "Your dog?" she said.

"No, I just found him on the subway," I said. "He followed me here. He seems to like your little boy."

"My son Alexei had a dog just like this one,"

she said. "His name was Danya. He died a couple of months ago. Alexei loved him so."

"You know," I said, and hesitated. I really wanted to take that dog back home with me. But I knew that wasn't practical. Misha belonged here in Russia with a little boy who would love him.

"I can't take this dog back to America with me," I said. "Would you like to have him? I know you'll take good care of him and your little boy will love him."

"Is true?" she said, her whole face reflecting her joy. She leaned down and said something to her son in Russian. He reached up and hugged her and then put his arms around Misha, whose tail was wagging so furiously I thought it would knock somebody over.

"Thank you," the lady said. "I can see by your face how much you love him. I make picture for you." She took out her phone and took a picture of my dog and sent it to my phone.

"I send you more when I get home," she said. "You will see how much we love him, that he is happy with Alexei."

I thanked her and knelt down to hug my Misha good-bye. He licked my face and smiled at me and then turned back to Alexei. It was as if he knew which one of us needed him the most.

There were tears in my eyes when I joined my friends again.

"You OK, hon?" Mary Louise asked me as we took our seats in the theater.

"I guess," I said, but I knew I would never forget that big friendly dog, whose generous nature seemed to embody everything good about Russia.

The house lights dimmed. The music blared and the ringmaster appeared in a large spotlight with nine tigers. Magnificent orange-brown beasts with black markings, they moved restlessly back and forth, their regal faces turning side to side. At a crack of the whip, the tigers jumped through a large flaming hoop one by one, filling the air with the noise of their snarling and growling.

"Aren't they gorgeous?" Mary Louise said. "Are they an endangered species?"

"Yes, I read that all tigers are endangered now," I said, missing my sweet little tortoiseshell cat, Pandora, who was probably taking a nap on the windowsill back home.

Pandora had kept me sane and functioning in the months following Bill's death. I would climb into bed and she would jump up to snuggle next to me. Don't get me wrong. A cat can't make up for a man next to you in bed, but she's the next best thing. Just patting her silky fur and holding her on my lap when I'm feeling sad and lonely helps a lot. I love her. And love always works miracles.

The tigers got a standing ovation. When the

ring was cleared, five acrobats swung from trapezes, gliding through the air, jumping down into the net, climbing up to high platforms, and sailing gracefully to grasp the hands of their partners. Jugglers, clowns, equestrians, and tightrope walkers dazzled us with their amazing skills.

After the show was over, we filed out to our bus, where Andrei was waiting for us.

Just as I was about to get on the coach, I felt something bump against my leg. Misha had come to say good-bye to me. I knelt down to hug him. Alexei and his mother stood nearby smiling as they watched that big dog lick my face with farewell kisses.

"Take good care of Alexei, Misha. Keep him safe," I said, trying not to cry. "You're a good dog," I said to Misha.

He gave my arm one more nudge and walked back to Alexei.

"*Dasvidaniya*, nice lady," the little boy said. I waved good-bye to him as I climbed on the bus.

Mary Louise handed me a tissue as I sat next to her. "You did the right thing, sweetie," she said. "Did you see that little boy's face?"

"I know," I said, sniffing. "But I love that dog."

Gini reached over the seat and kissed the top of my head.

"How you like our circus?" Andrei asked. "Is best in world, no?"

"It was wonderful, Andrei," we said, and plopped back into our seats for the ride back to the ship.

If I had known what was waiting for me, I would have joined the circus instead.

Tina's Travel Tip: Morse code for "help" is three dots, three dashes, and three dots. Good luck finding someone else who knows what that means.

Chapter 22

Who Took My Lysol?

We decided to dress up for our last dinner on board.

I wore my white silk pantsuit with a black and white lace camisole and my black and white strappy high heels. Mary Louise looked gorgeous in a pale yellow dress with skinny shoulder straps.

We headed up the stairs to the dining room when I realized I'd forgotten something.

"You go ahead," I said. "I just want to get my black art deco earrings from the top shelf. I'll be right with you."

I ran back to the cabin and stood on the bed to reach my earrings when I heard a faint sound in the bathroom. I froze. No, it must be next door, I thought, and hopped off the bed.

The bathroom door opened. I couldn't believe what I saw. This must be some kind of nightmare, I thought. It can't be who I think it is. But there, pointing a gun at me and grinning evilly, was the chef. Ken Allgood.

"You're not dead," I stammered. It was all I could think of to say.

"Brilliant," he said. "I made sure there's no Lysol in here, so don't even think about pulling another spray-and-run."

"That was you with the scarf around your head?" I said. "You sounded like a Russian."

"Pretty good, huh? It would have worked too, if you hadn't gotten lucky with that can of Lysol."

"How did you get in here?" I said. "We were changing into our dinner clothes only a minute ago."

"I was under the bed behind the life jackets," he said. "I've been here all day. I have a score to settle with you, sweetheart, and this time you're getting me off this ship."

"How are you going to do that with police all over the ship?" I said.

"Once they see you tap-tapping down the corridor with a gun to your head, they'll do whatever I tell them."

This couldn't be happening again. I might have gotten away from him once, but how was I going to do it twice? My hands were sweating, I felt faint, but I had to hold on. Stay calm, I told myself. Don't panic. You're smarter than this jerk. Yeah, but he's got the gun, I realized. A gun trumps brains any day.

"But they pulled your body from the river," I said. "How could you . . ."

"That wasn't my body, honey," he said.

"Whose was it?"

"You ask too many questions."

"What's the difference? If you're going to kill me, you might as well tell me."

"I have other plans for you, sweetheart."

I suddenly understood the expression, "my blood ran cold."

"Whose body was it?" I asked again, trying to stall him.

"It was that American boy."

"You mean Brad Sheldon?"

"Yeah, yeah. Who else?"

"Did you kill him?" I asked.

"What do you think?"

"But why? You had no reason to hurt him."

"I had a very good reason. He wouldn't give me what I wanted."

"What was that?" I had to keep him talking, stall for time until I could figure out what to do.

"His passport. Why else would I bother with someone the same height, same color hair, same age as me? I had to pretend to have the hots for him to get him into my room. I almost threw up when I had to kiss him. But it was the only way I could get him to help me get to New York. I'll do anything to get there, including killing you if you don't do what I tell you."

"We thought you were bisexual because of that young girl you kissed," I said, trying to think of anything to say, to keep him answering instead of shooting me. "She's underage, you know. You could have been in big trouble."

"I've been in trouble all my life, sweetie. Anyway, Sheldon told me he would help me get to New York and that I could stay with him and he would introduce me to some people in the restaurant business. He lied—the little rat. He weaseled out of the whole deal and told me he didn't know anybody in the restaurant business and that he couldn't help me. He said it would be best if we didn't see each other anymore. I knew I had to act fast, so after I saw that he had his American passport on him when he cashed a check, I told him we could at least have one last drink together in my room, no hard feelings, and the dummy agreed. I don't know why I'm telling you all this. You're too nosy."

"Who am I going to tell? You might as well tell me what happened."

"Yeah, why not?" He laughed. "I put some knockout drops in his drink and then I strangled him and took his passport. Before he passed out, he struggled a lot and I had to hit him a few times. There was blood all over the place. I put my jacket on him, stuck my British passport in a plastic pouch and placed it in the pocket of the jacket, and threw his body overboard. With his passport, I can start over in New York. I've had enough of jolly old England and Mother Russia to last me a lifetime. Nobody will miss him."

"Well, why did you shoot Sasha?" I asked. What did he do?"

"Oh, that twit! I sneaked out in the middle of the night to get something to eat in the kitchen and Sasha came in to do something. I never did figure out what he did on this ship. Anyway, he saw me in there and I had to shoot him. I tried to drag him out to the deck and throw him overboard, but he was too heavy. I only got as far as the top of the stairs where you and your pals found him."

"Why are you still on the ship if you have Brad's passport? Why didn't you just go?"

"How am I gonna do that, honey? They check you coming and going on this ship. I can't swim back to shore, now can I? As long as this gun is pointed at you, they won't stop me from getting off the ship. I keep you with me until I can get to the garage where I left my rental car before the cruise. Once away from the police, I'll leave good old Mother Russia. You don't need to know how I'll do that or where I'm going. You just be a good girl and do as you're told until I'm off the ship and you can go back to your tap dancing. Any trouble out of you and you're dead."

"You can't really think you'll get away with this," I said. "The Russian police won't care what happens to me. They'll shoot you down and if I get killed, tough."

"Bad for the tourist business if you get killed, cutie," he said. "You're semi-famous. They won't want that kind of publicity."

"So when are you going to do this?" I said, wondering what was holding me together.

"Ten minutes and then we're out of here."

"Whatever made you decide to become a chef when you can't cook?" I asked, saying anything I could think of to keep him talking.

"You don't know anything," he said, glaring at me. "I went to one of the best cooking schools in England. I would have been fine if they hadn't made me cook that Russian slop."

"Well, why did you take a job cooking on a Russian cruise ship, then?"

"It was the only job I could get. I was working in a crummy little place in London, but they wanted me to be a lousy sous-chef—standing around in that sweaty kitchen cutting up carrots and onions and celery, doing all the crap the main cook didn't want to do. He was from some African country and he didn't know anything about food. I made such a stink about him, I was fired. My stupid brother-in-law who works in the London office of this cruise line got me a job on this ship just to get rid of me. That's when I made up my mind I was going to get to America, where you can get a decent job and good pay. In New York City, there's a restaurant every couple of feet. With an American passport, nobody's going to ask me any questions. I'll work there until I get my own place."

"You didn't have to kill anyone to get to New York," I said, trying to edge closer to the door. "You could have gotten a visa and worked there. Eventually, you could become an American citizen."

"I tried that! But I have a record. I was in juvenile detention from the time I was fifteen until I was twenty, when I was a kid in Manchester. They said I was selling drugs, but I only gave some to my friends, and they put me in that stinkin' place. After I got out of there, I got sent away for robbing a liquor store."

"So you're going to change your name to Brad Sheldon?" I said. "The police will know you have his passport. They'll find you if you get a social security card under that name or sign anything with his name. You'll be hunted down for the rest of your life for these two murders."

"Or three murders *if you don't do what I say*," he said, thrusting his gun forward. "Once I get over there, I won't need his name anymore. I'll take another name and just disappear. There are ways to get fake working papers anywhere, and I know how to do it. Anyway, it's none of your business what I do. You're my ticket out of here. The less you open your yap, the better I'll like it. Enough chitchat, baby. We're leaving."

"You're going to miss a great routine," I said, improvising with the first thing that came to mind. "For our final performance, we're doing a whole routine from *Chorus Line*. You know, *One singular sensation . . .*" I swung into a tap-tap-tap, stomp-stomp-stomp, tap-tap-tap step, which I hoped was the Morse code for SOS. I really didn't know why I was doing this. The chances of anyone even hearing me, much less someone who knew Morse code, were nonexistent.

"Now that you're almost an American, you should learn some American show tunes," I babbled on. "That's the way people really know you're an American." I sounded ridiculous even to myself.

"I'll have plenty of time to learn American songs when I'm in New York. Anyway, your dancing is terrible," he said. "Why would I want to see you do more of that?"

"Come on, give me a chance to prove you're wrong," I said with a smile. I started to sing the words to "Singin' in the Rain" as loudly as I could. At the same time, I tap-tap-tapped, stomp-stomp-

stomped, tap-tap-tapped. I flung my arms out, and he brought his gun closer.

"Shut up with the singing. It's worse than your dancing," he said.

I hummed, instead. And tapped and stomped in threes, praying that someone would hear me and realize what I was doing. I couldn't think of anything else to do since I'd already used up my Lysol escape. When in doubt, tap, I always say.

"That's enough," he said. "We're getting out of here, so move your butt. I'm right behind you with this gun, so don't try anything funny."

He opened the door slowly, making sure there was nobody in the corridor, and pushed me ahead of him toward the exit. I walked as slowly as I could, holding onto the wall.

"Hurry up," he said. "You can walk faster than that."

"My legs are all wobbly," I said. I pretended to cry. "I can't walk any faster. Please, let me sit down for a minute."

"Shut up and walk." He shoved me and I fell forward on my knees. He tripped over me and held onto the railing in the corridor to keep from falling. Then suddenly somebody grabbed me and covered my body with his. I heard the gun go off, but I couldn't see what was happening because my face was pressed to the floor. There was the sound of scuffling and a body dropped to the floor.

I heard a mixture of Russian and English, and I could see men's feet all around me. I didn't move.

"Put your hands behind your back," I heard, then, a lot of Russian words as the police officers shoved Allgood against the wall.

Whoever was on top of me smelled very familiar, but I didn't dare move to see who it was. A voice said in my ear, "Tina, darling, are you all right?"

"Peter, is that you? What are you doing here? Am I still alive? Where's Allgood?"

Peter turned me right side up and held me in his arms so tightly, I almost couldn't breathe.

"You're all right, honey. The police shot Allgood in the leg. They're taking him off the ship."

"How did you get here? What are you doing here? I tried to call you but you didn't answer. Did you get my message?"

Peter brushed a stray curl back from my face. "I booked a flight as soon as you told me there had been a murder on the ship. I went to St. Petersburg first because I thought you were there. Turned out the ship had sailed to Moscow. I rented a car and drove here as fast as I could— it's three hundred miles—and just got here now."

His brown eyes were full of worry.

"I'll never forget you did this for me," I said, pressing my face against his chest.

"When I got to the pier, there were police officers everywhere," he continued. "I found one who spoke pretty good English and asked him what was going on. He told me they were looking for the chef's murderer, who had held you at gunpoint back in St. Petersburg. Tina, how could you not tell me that?"

"I didn't want to worry you, Peter. I got away from him by spraying him with Lysol. I was sure he had left the ship." I knew I was babbling again, but I couldn't stop.

"From now on, feel free to worry me. I want to know anytime someone points a gun at you!"

I looked at his face, this face I had seen so many times, and realized how attractive he was. Was what I was feeling for him now love? Or just gratitude that he had saved my life?

"Oh, Peter, I'm so glad to see you," I said, holding onto him tightly. "But how did you know where I was?"

"I ran into Mary Louise. She said you went back to the cabin and told me your room number. I got to the corridor and I heard you tapping in Morse code."

"I can't believe that Morse code you taught me saved my life," I said. "I never dreamed that I'd have to use it—much less that you would be the one to hear it."

"Good thing I learned it in Boy Scouts for one of my badges."

"What badge was that—the Rescuing Damsels in Distress badge?"

"Anyway, I was just about to pound on your door, when I heard a man's voice telling you to get moving. I ran for the police, who were right outside on the deck. They tackled the guy when you tripped him, and I pushed you to the floor. He tried to get away. They shot him in the leg."

"Oh, Peter, you could have been killed."

"All I could think of was getting you away from him," Peter said, his voice breaking. "I couldn't stand it if anything happened to you."

I was crying too hard to answer him.

After the police took Allgood off the ship, my friends came running down the stairs.

"I knew I should have stayed with you," Mary Louise said.

"Oh, Tina—we thought you'd been shot," Pat said.

"Can we go somewhere and sit down?" Peter said. "I'm a little weak in the knees."

"There's a bar on the top deck," Gini said.

"I could use a drink," he said, still holding me. "Tina, can you walk OK?"

"If I can lean on you. I'm not sure my legs are working."

"Hang on, kid."

The Skylight Bar was filled with people who had heard what happened. When they saw me come through the door, they surrounded me to see if I was all right.

"Tina, we heard shots. Are you OK?" Mark said.

I told him Allgood was the only one shot and that I was fine. A little shaky, but not wounded.

I told my friends what Allgood had told me about Brad Sheldon and why he killed him.

Janice covered her face. "Oh, that poor boy," she said. "I should have made sure he didn't go to Allgood's cabin. He had nobody to look after him. I should have protected him."

"I don't think anyone could have kept him from going to Ken's cabin, Jan," Pat said. "He was lonely. Allgood seemed to offer what he needed."

"I could have tried," she said.

"You did try," I said. "I heard you." I put my arms around her.

Caroline grabbed my hand. "Tina, we thought you had been killed. Oh, my dear, I'm so glad you're all right."

Stacy and Andrea came up for a group hug.

Alex, who was holding onto Gini as if he were afraid she would disappear, said, "Tina . . ." For once, he was speechless, but I could see the relief on his face.

Heidi was so glad to see that I was safe, she actually patted me on the head. "*Ach!*" was all she could manage. "But what did he tell you about Mr. Sheldon? Is he still alive?"

I took another sip of my drink and I told Heidi the story.

"The chef is still alive?" Heidi said, totally confused. "He didn't kill himself because I threatened to fire him?"

"No, Heidi, he killed Brad," I said, and tried to tell her more clearly what the chef had told me.

"*Ach*," Heidi said, still confused. "He had a gun. He could have killed you."

"He's under arrest now," Alex assured her.

Stacy let go of her grandmother's hand and pulled me over to the side. "Tina, that could have been me. I almost went to his cabin. He seemed so nice. I mean, I kissed him! And he's a murderer." She started to cry.

I put my arms around her. "Your passport wouldn't have done him much good, Stacy. He wouldn't have killed you."

"I'll never kiss anybody again," she said.

"Oh, yes, you will," I said. "Don't start thinking that every man you meet is a possible murderer. Most of them are just boring—not murderers."

She laughed and wiped away the tears and went back to her grandmother.

"Are you all right, honey?" Caroline asked her granddaughter. "Didn't Andrea say something about you and the chef? He gave you a tour of the ship or something?"

Stacy glared at her sister over her grandmother's head. "I really didn't know him very well, Nana."

Her grandmother looked at me. She'd been in this world for eighty years, after all.

"That's good, dear," she said to Stacy. "I know you always tell me the truth."

Stacy looked like she was about to cry again.

The Russian waitresses tried to express their sympathy with body language. Olga covered her face and mimed crying. She put her hand over her heart. I smiled and said, "*Spasiba.*" She attempted a "You're welcome." We had connected.

Barry pushed through the crowd around me and said, "Tina, are you all right. I'm here now. You're safe—"

Peter moved between me and Barry and said, "Hello, Barry."

"Peter? Peter Simpson? What are you doing here?" Barry took a step backward.

"Almost getting killed. I'm a friend of Tina's. I flew here from New York when I heard there had been a murder on the ship."

"I did my best to take care of her," Barry said.

"Shoulda tried a little harder, Barry," Gini said, and he glared at her.

"Well, I'm here now," he said. "I'll make sure she's all right."

Peter put his arm around me and said quietly,

"I don't think so, Barry. From now on, that's my job."

"*Dasvidaniya*, Barry," Gini said. "So long and don't let the door hit you as you leave."

Barry started to say something, but seeing himself surrounded by hostile stares, he turned and left the bar.

Heidi came over to our group again.

"If you think you can eat, Sergei has prepared a feast for your last night on this ship."

"Sounds good to me," Peter said. "I can't remember the last time I ate. I've been trying to get here for days and I didn't want to take time for food."

"Poor baby," I said. "Come with me."

I tottered to my feet and headed for the dining room, holding on to Peter, when Tatiana ran over to hug me. "Tina. Are you all right?" she said. "I heard you were shot."

"No, I'm all in one piece, for now," I said. "Tatiana, this is my friend Peter. He crossed oceans and forged rivers to save me."

Tatiana shook his hand. "I'm so glad. We all love Tina."

Peter just looked at me. "Yes," he said. "We do."

"Tatiana, please have dinner with us."

I saw Sue and Mark and Caroline and her granddaughters nearby. "Come on, you guys. You have to join us for our last dinner on the ship."

Chapter 23

Tina's Travel Tips You Can Really Use

Heidi had several tables pushed against each other so we could all sit together. I sat down, holding tightly to Peter's hand.

"Would you mind if I gave thanks?" Caroline said when we were all seated in a circle.

"Please, Caroline," I said. "Please do."

We all bowed our heads, even our atheist, Gini.

"Thank you for keeping us all safe and for watching over our Tina," Caroline said. "Thank you for giving us another day to enjoy every breath we take, every mouthful we eat, every friend we cherish, every time we get to say I love you." She paused, and then smiled at me. "And for another chance to put on our tap shoes. Amen."

"Amen, Caroline. See you at Macy's next Tap-a-thon."

Olga brought our first course and actually smiled as she served it.

"What is this, Olga?" Gini asked.

"Blinis with sevruga and salmon caviar," she said proudly.

One taste and we were all clinking our water glasses with our spoons and chanting, "Chef, chef, chef."

Tatiana ran into the kitchen and came out dragging a reluctant Sergei.

"Sergei, this is just perfect," Janice said.

Sergei blushed, and said something to Titiana in Russian.

"Sergei says thank you, but wait until you taste his main course of sautéed prawns in saffron sauce with a seafood risotto."

We all cheered and an embarrassed Sergei retreated into the safety of his kitchen.

"So, my American friends," Tatiana said, "what do you think of my country?"

We were all quiet for a minute, trying to think of a way to sum up this complicated, fascinating country.

"We saw things we would never see anywhere else," Sue said. "Mark and I have traveled a lot, Tatiana, but Russia is so different from all the other places we've been—especially Europe, where most people speak English, and we could figure out the language better."

"It's the Cyrillic alphabet," Mark said. "We can't read the signs and most people don't speak English, so it felt strange. But that's why we love to travel. To see and hear and taste things we'd never experience at home."

"I was impressed with the beauty of the cathedrals and palaces in St. Petersburg," Sue said. "We grew up with a whole different impression of Russia."

"Yes," Mark said. "We were expecting no frills. You know—no nonsense. Just work and no dancing or singing or beauty."

"And now?" Tatiana asked.

"We saw beauty everywhere," Janice said. "In the colors of your clothes. In the theater—the plush maroon seats, the gold chandeliers. I loved seeing the velvet and ermine clothes of the tsars in the Armoury—and I especially loved those Fabergé eggs. They were exquisitely made."

"I thought St. Petersburg was one of the most beautiful cities I've ever seen," I said. "I always thought Paris was the most exquisite city in the world, but St. Petersburg—with all those canals and the palaces, the modern buildings, the rich cultural life—is almost as lovely."

"Hey, Tina," Pat said, "you're writing about this trip for your magazine, right? What kind of travel tips will you give your honeymooners who might decide to do this?"

"First of all, they should carry a can of Lysol spray everywhere they go, in case they meet a murderer," I said, and there was a loud burst of laughter from all my friends.

"No, seriously," I continued, "I already made my list of things to do and not do if you take this trip to Russia. Want to hear them?"

"Yes, please," Stacy said. "One of them should be: Don't kiss the chef—he might turn out to be a killer."

"You kissed the chef?" Caroline said. "When did you do that?"

"Oh, I meant to tell you about that, Nana," Stacy said. "I'll explain later."

Caroline rolled her eyes. "Go ahead Tina. What else?"

"I'm not putting this in the article, but it might be a good idea to make sure there's a Russian chef in the kitchen," I said. "But here are the tips I'm using in the article:

- "• Make copies of your passport, airline tickets, credit card numbers, insurance information, and any other important travel documents, and put them in a separate envelope in case the originals are lost or stolen on the trip.
- "• You need a visa to go to Russia, so be sure and get it way ahead of time.
- "• For a trip to Russia, your passport must be valid for six months following your trip.
- "• Make sure the name on your airline ticket is exactly the same as the name on your

passport or they might not let you on the ship.

"• You should check flight times seventy-two hours in advance, because international flight times can change at any time."

"These are really good tips, Tina," Mary Louise said. "Especially for honeymooners. There are so many things to do before the wedding, you might not realize you have to do all that stuff."

"What else are you telling them?" Sue asked. "These are really helpful."

"Are you going to tell them about using their cell phones?" Stacy asked. "I could use mine some of the time but not always."

"Good point, Stacy. I'll put it in the article: You can make or get calls from home when the ship is in a port with good reception. There will be times when you won't be able to get calls, but you can get a toll-free number from the cruise line for your family if they need to call you. And be sure you give anyone who might try to call you the right code, because it's different when you're calling overseas."

"How about clothes?" Andrea asked. "What will you tell them to bring? I wasn't sure."

"You always look great, Andrea," I said. "But you're right. Nobody really knows what to wear in Russia. I'll add this: Basically, you should bring the same things you would wear on any cruise, but you need to bring some sweaters or jackets, because it's always colder on a ship than walking around a city. Especially if your wedding is in the spring or fall."

"Should you bring dressy clothes?"

"Most of the time you can wear casual clothes—nothing sloppy—but nice casual. And you might want to dress up for dinner once or twice."

"What about the men?" Mark asked. "Are you telling them to bring ties and jackets?"

"On this ship they're not necessary, but some men do wear a jacket to dinner."

"We're talking about young men, presumably—since it's their honeymoon. Do young men need to bring jackets?"

"Well," I said, "I wouldn't tell them to go out and buy one just for the trip. But if they have one, they might as well bring it along."

"What are you telling them about packing?" Janice asked. "Got any good tips for that? I was really glad you told me to pack my dresses in dry cleaner's plastic bags. You can fold them up a couple of times and the plastic keeps them from wrinkling. Anything else like that?"

"Just don't bring too much," I said. "That's the main thing. But I wanted to tell them some things they should bring that they may not have thought about."

"I could have used that before I left," Pat said. "I forgot Band-Aids."

"Band-Aids are good for blisters, or if you get a minor cut," I said. "Also, be sure and bring shoes you've walked in a lot—not new ones. And pack some nice ones to wear to a restaurant in town. You also need an umbrella, sun block, and sunglasses, and bring pills in case you catch a cold, get diarrhea, or have a headache. If you go in the middle of summer, you might want a mosquito repellent."

"I forgot to bring an electrical converter and plug adapter for my hair dryer and Mark's electric razor," Sue said. "Mark bought a regular razor here, but he wanted to use his own."

"That's good, Sue," I said. "I'll be sure to remind them of that. Also, an alarm clock you can see in the dark and a sewing kit in case you rip something. There are tons of other things I'm going to put in, but one more that's essential is how to avoid jet lag, since there's a six hour difference in time. You should eat lightly, don't drink too much liquor or coffee. Drink lots of water and fruit juice during the flight. Try to sleep on an overnight flight if you can. Even a nap is better than staying awake the whole time. Walk around and stretch. When you arrive, don't sleep right away. Stay awake until nighttime if you can."

"Really useful, Tina," Caroline said. "I'm telling everyone to buy your magazine before they go anywhere."

"Love you, Caroline," I said.

"They really are good tips, Tina," Alex said. "Even *I* learned something, and I travel all the time. I think I'll be making a lot more trips to New York from now on." He looked at Gini, and we all knew what he meant.

"How much longer will you be in Moscow, Alex?" I asked.

"I'm thinking of leaving very soon," he said, smiling at Gini. "I want to be back in New York again. I've been here for two years now and the *Times* has offered me the chance to return to the New York office. I'm really looking forward to the change. I'll get to see new places . . ."

"Like India?" Gini asked.

"Like India," Alex said. "I'd like to do a story on their adoption policy there. I think they make it much too difficult for Americans, for example, to adopt one of their children."

Gini looked at me as if to say, "This is definitely the man for me." I nodded. I thought so too.

"I'm curious," I said. "I'd love to know what our two teenagers think of Russia. Did you have a good time?"

"Oh yes!" Stacy said. "Especially when you let us dance in your act. That was so neat. I'm going to do more tap dancing when I get back."

"I was surprised to find that kids here know so much about American music and movies and video games," Andrea said. "I thought they hated us, but when we talked to them in the shops and on the street—some of them spoke pretty good English—they wanted to know all about Lindsay Lohan and Miley Cyrus and Justin Bieber. They asked us where we got our jeans and if they could buy any from us. We should have brought along about ten extra pairs."

"But would you want to live here?"

"No way," Stacy said. "They have no money. I realized how spoiled we are in our country, where kids have cars and cell phones and TVs and computers without even realizing how lucky they are."

"It's different now, though, since Soviet system is finished," Tatiana said. "I have two daughters. They are at the university and they can do pretty much whatever they like when they finish. They both want to make money, but they also have a real appreciation of the culture of our country, and they want to do something that will help other people. They want to be doctors, but it's too soon to tell if they can do it."

"You certainly showed them what a woman can do," Janice said. "With two PhDs and a career teaching at the university and lecturing all over the world and on cruise ships."

"This was my first cruise that included two murders," Tatiana said. "Very exciting, but I could do without that the next time."

"Me too!" I said. "Especially since I was to be one of the murderees."

Mary McHugh

Olga brought us course after course of incredible food with superb wines.

I looked around the table at all these new friends and old friends.

"Let's try to stay in touch," I said. "It would be a shame to live through two murders, two attempted abductions, a circus, and a thirty-second viewing of Leonardo da Vinci's *Madonna and Child* together and not send each other an e-mail every once in a while when life happens."

"Great idea," Mark said. "Do you Hoofers know where you're going to be dancing next? What other part of the world will you be bringing mayhem to?"

"We haven't decided yet," I said.

"Wherever you go, let us know," Sue said. "We'll be there."

We all promised to stay in touch and exchange e-mails. Tatiana said she would try to stop and see us on her way to her next lecture tour, which was in California. Alex kissed Gini and obviously didn't want to let her go. "I'll be in New York soon," he said. "In the meantime, write me, call me, tell me what's happening with your little girl."

"I will, Alex," Gini said. "I'll see you soon."

I was suddenly exhausted.

"Peter, I have to go to bed. It's all catching up with me. Where will you sleep tonight?" I asked.

"If you think I'm leaving you alone after chasing you for days and you almost getting killed, you're crazy. I'm not leaving you for one second. I'll just sleep on the other bunk in your cabin, and Mary Louise, maybe you wouldn't mind bunking in with Gini for one night?"

"Of course I don't mind," Mary Louise said. "Gini, is that OK with you?"

"More than OK," Gini said. "I may sleep somewhere else anyway." She smiled.

"I have a feeling everyone else on this cruise is having a lot more fun than I am," Mary Louise said.

I said good night to everyone and Peter held my hand until we got to the cabin.

When I woke up the next morning, Peter was gone. The shower floor was wet. I figured he must have dressed and gone to breakfast. But soon there was a soft tap at the door. I opened it to see him holding a tray of croissants, hot chocolate, and a mushroom omelet.

"Good morning," he said, looking fresh and adorable in a black shirt and white pants.

"Oh, thank you, Peter, this is perfect. How did you know I would rather have hot chocolate than coffee or tea?"

"When you and Bill came up to our house on the Cape while I was still married to Marian, you asked for hot chocolate at breakfast. I remembered, that's all."

I smiled at him. It was so good to have him in my life.

There was a knock at the door.

"Tina," Mary Louise said. "We're meeting in the dining room for one last breakfast before the bus takes us to the airport. Are you coming?"

"We'll be there in a minute," I said, taking a bite of croissant and a sip of cocoa.

I dressed and we joined the others in the dining room.

After breakfast, we said our good-byes to Caroline and Stacy and Andrea.

"Always do what you love," Pat said to the girls.

"*Dasvidaniya*, Hoofers," Caroline said, giving me a hug.

"Let's meet at the Frick Collection soon," Sue said to me.

Heidi was standing at the head of the ramp as we left.

"Good-bye, Happy Hoofers," she said. "It was a pleasure having you on this cruise. I'm glad you are all right, Ms. Powell."

"I trust Ken Allgood is safely in jail," I said.

"Oh yes. Do not worry. He will be in prison for a long, long time."

"What about Brad Sheldon?" Janice asked. "His poor parents."

"They are here now, arranging to have his body sent back to the States."

"He was a sweet boy," Janice said.

We walked down the ramp. Just before we got on the bus, Mary Louise, Janice, Pat, Gini, and I linked arms and did a few high kicks to say goodbye to the *Smirnov*.

Chapter 24

Home Sweet Home

After *The Times* ran the story of my rescue from the murderer, we got lots of offers to perform.

One of my daughters was appalled, the other one envious.

"Mother!" Laurie said when she met me at the airport in Newark. "You could have been killed."

"But I wasn't, darling. And we're going to dance in a lot more exotic places, so get used to it."

"I'll never keep up with you, Mom. But I hope I'm just like you when I'm fifty-three."

My other daughter, Kyle, called me the minute I got in the house.

"Mom! You should have taken me along. I could have polished your tap shoes or something. How could you go on an adventure like that and not take me with you?"

"Honey, I had no idea I was going to be mixed

up in a murder and an abduction and an evil chef. Or I would have taken you."

"I'll be home this weekend," she said. "And you can tell me all about it."

When my friends and I met at Starbucks two days later, everyone had news.

"Sandy and I have started working on the book," Janice said. "I'm so glad to have her back in my life again."

"I heard from Alex," Gini said. "He's coming back to New York to work and he's arranging for us to go to India together."

"George was so glad I was back home safe and unhurt, he took me out to dinner," Mary Louise said.

"He was just glad to see you so you can resume your cooking and cleaning," Janice said.

"He's taking me to Paris for a second honeymoon," Mary Louise said triumphantly, "so he can keep an eye on me and make sure I'm not murdered."

"I have some news too," I said, smiling broadly.

"Tell us," Mary Louise said.

"We have an offer to dance on a luxury train traveling across northern Spain!"

"When?"

"Who hired us?"

"How much?"

"Is the chef British?"

"Did you say yes?"

"We go in September if you're game. The

Spanish Tourist Board wants us. They'll pay us a really good fee. I said I couldn't say yes until I'd talked to all of you."

Gini wasn't sure she wanted to be away from Alex so soon after he'd transferred to New York. Mary Louise didn't think George would let her out of the house without him again. Pat was afraid there'd be another murder. Janice was booked to direct a play in Morristown. And I was supposed to go to the Cape with Peter.

So naturally we decided to go.

Want to come along?

Don't miss the next Happy Hoofers mystery
FLAMENCO, FLAN, AND FATALITIES
Documentary filmmaker Gini Miller takes over
as narrator as the Happy Hoofers solve a
murder mystery in Spain . . .
Coming from Kensington in March 2015

Keep reading for an enticing preview excerpt . . .

Chapter 1

Buen Apetito!

I must say, the five of us were a good-looking group in our silky summer dresses and strappy high heels, earrings swinging, as we strolled toward the coach that would take us to the restaurant for dinner.

We climbed aboard and said hello to the other passengers from our luxury train. It was our first night in Spain, and we couldn't wait to see everything, do everything, experience everything in this amazing country. We took seats in two available rows and craned our necks, looking out the windows at the bustling street in front of the station.

Just as the door closed and the driver gunned the engine into life, there was a loud commotion. We heard a familiar voice demanding that the bus wait for him. I looked out and saw a large, sweaty man waving his arms and shouting.

"Where is Eduardo?" he yelled. "He was supposed to make all the arrangements for me on the train. Where is he?"

I'd heard this voice before somewhere. A strong wave of dislike grabbed me. Who was this person? Why didn't I like him?

"Nobody knows how to do anything in this country," he said.

Eduardo, the host of our train trip across northern Spain, got off the bus and held out his hand to the noisy man.

"I'm so sorry, Mr. Shambless. I'm Eduardo. We waited for you and your party as long as we could. We have reservations for dinner and we have to leave on time." Our host was slender and dapper in dark slacks and a starched white shirt. The shouter, by contrast, looked like an unmade bed.

"I'm filming this whole trip on your crowded little train for my TV show. I'd have thought you'd have the decency to wait for me and my crew before you ran off to the restaurant. They'll wait for us. They can't buy publicity like my show will give them. And neither can you.' He waved a pudgy finger in Eduardo's face, as if he were not the center of attention already.

"We are indeed grateful that you chose our trip, Mr. Shambless," Eduardo said. I cringed, watching this nice man having to acquiesce to this creep. "I regret any confusion I may have caused. Please join us on the bus and tell me what I can do to help you."

"Just stay out of my way unless I need you," Shambless said, motioning to his cameraman and to a pretty young woman. The woman had long, straight blond hair and a V-neck blouse that showed off her incredible breasts every time she bent over, which was often.

I remembered why I disliked this man the minute I heard his voice. Dick Shambless was a television talk show host who enthralled whole sections of the country every day with his anti-gay, antigovernment, anti-everything rantings. Why did he have to come on this trip?

One of the women sitting near us stood up and pulled the man sitting next to her to a seat in the back of the coach. I heard her say, "I don't want to talk to him," as she moved to the last row.

"Just ignore him, Sylvia," the man said, settling next to her with a camera bag on his lap. "You don't have to be afraid of him anymore."

I nudged my friend Mary Louise, who was leafing through a brochure about local attractions.

"Did you see the look on that woman's face when she heard Shambless's voice?" I whispered to her.

She looked up, concern in her lovely blue eyes. "Yes, Gini. She seemed—I don't know—angry? Scared? What was it?"

"Well, she certainly wasn't happy to see him."

The talk show guy lurched onto the bus, heaving his vast weight into the front seat, without a hello or how are you to anybody around him. The cameraman stood in the front of the bus and filmed Shambless and then swung the camera around to include the rest of us.

Eduardo leaned over closer to Shambless and said, "You might want to include our beautiful dancers, who are going to entertain us on this trip. Our Happy Hoofers."

"Happy Hookers?" Shambless said. "Why would I want to include a bunch of hookers?"

"No, no," Eduardo said, embarrassed, looking at us apologetically. "They're dancers and we are really lucky to have them."

"Tell them to stand up," Shambless said. "Let me get a look at these babes."

Eduardo asked each of us to stand. We reluctantly got to our feet as he introduced us individually. I was ready to slug Shambless, but I felt sorry for Eduardo, so I smiled into the camera when he said, "This is Gini Miller, award-winning filmmaker and dancer extraordinaire."

Eduardo asked Tina to stand next. "And this is Tina Powell, magazine editor and leader of the dancers."

Shambless snorted when Eduardo motioned to Janice to stand. "Janice Rogers, actress and director," Eduardo said.

"You sure that's hoofers with an *f?*" Shambless

aid. I was about to punch his lights out when he man with Sylvia shouted out, "Janice! Janice Rogers. I didn't know you were on this trip."

He pushed his way down the aisle to hug her.

"Janice Rogers," he said. "I don't believe you're here. It's so good to see you again. How are you? Are you still acting?"

Janice pulled away to look at him.

"Tom Carson," she said. "It must be ten years since we were in 'Who's Afraid of Virginia Woolf' in New York. How are you? Are you still acting?"

"If you can call it that. I'm in a soap opera. I haven't been in anything on the stage in years."

"Listen, nothing wrong with soaps. It's still acting. Which one are you in?"

"Love in the Afternoon," he said. "Have you ever seen it?"

"I have seen it actually," she said. "In fact, it's really good. I got hooked on it one year when I didn't have an acting job and was just sitting around waiting for the phone to ring."

"Can we get on with this?" Shambless said impatiently. "You can sleep with her later."

I would have killed him right then and there, but the man said, "We'll catch up at dinner, Jan," and went back to his seat.

Eduardo introduced Pat as a family therapist and Mary Louise as "the mother of three," and the cameraman finished filming us.

As the bus started, the nicely stacked blonde

sat down next to Shambless and turned on a tape recorder. He started to talk into it when a petite woman behind him leaned over his seat and said, "Oh, Mr. Shambless, I'm one of your biggest fans. I watch you every day and I thank God for all you do to protect our country. You're a national treasure."

He turned to her with a forced smile and said "God bless you. I'd be nothing without loyal fans like you." He patted her hand.

I felt like I was going to be sick, but I kept my mouth shut and muttered to Pat, sitting in front of me, "What is he doing here? He'll ruin the whole trip."

Pat turned around to say to me in a low voice, "We don't have to talk to him. In fact, please keep me from saying anything to him. He's a Neanderthal. He hates everything—intelligent women, gays, the president, social welfare programs—everything. I can never understand why so many people listen to him."

"I don't get that either," I said. "The few times I've heard him when I surf through the channels, I just wanted to strangle him."

"You'd make a lot of people happy if you did. Anyway, try to relax. Just ignore him and enjoy the ride."

"You're right, Pat, but it won't be easy."

On the way to the restaurant, our guide, a young Spanish woman named Rafaela, stood and picked up a microphone to give us a brief history of this part of Spain, or Green Spain, as it's called.

"Our train follows the five-hundred-mile route that pilgrims take from San Sebastian in the east to the cathedral in Santiago de Compostela in the west, where the bones of St. James are buried—only, we're going in the opposite direction. The legend is that his body was brought from Jerusalem to Santiago de Compostela and buried in a field. Then, nine hundred years later, someone found the bones and the cathedral was built around them. Pilgrims make the long journey to see them and are given a free room and meals when they arrive. If they make the pilgrimage when St. James Day falls on a Sunday, it's a holy year and all their sins are forgiven forever. They go directly to heaven."

"What a load of baloney," Shambless said. "You'd have to be a real idiot to believe that stuff. How far is this restaurant, anyway? I'm starving."

The whole coach fell into a silence so hostile you could touch it.

Rafaela looked at him, her dark eyes reflecting the anger most people in the bus were feeling. With admirable restraint, she said, "It's only a short distance. In fact, you can see it up the road there on the right."

I stood up to peer out the front window of the coach and saw a startlingly white stucco hacienda, surrounded by brilliant red oleander flowers, which were even more beautiful against the stark restaurant walls. I could see a sign reading EL GUSTO DEL MAR, which I think means "The Taste of the Sea." My Spanish isn't all that great.

When the bus pulled up to the gleaming white restaurant, Eduardo got off to shake hands with the owner, who was waiting to greet us. He was tall and handsome in the way that only Spanish men are—with that look in their eyes that says, "You cannot resist me."

"Ladies and gentlemen," Eduardo said, "I am pleased to introduce you to Señor Delgardo, the owner of El Gusto del Mar, this excellent restaurant."

Señor Delgardo smiled and held out his hand to Shambless, who was the first one of us to clamber out of the bus. The cameraman took pictures of the restaurant and the other buildings nearby. The blonde ignored the rest of us and put her arm through the talk show host's arm.

"Bienvenido, señor," Señor Delgardo said to him as he got off the bus. Shambless just grunted and pushed past him into the restaurant.

The rest of us tried to make up for his rudeness by shaking hands with the owner and telling him how much we were looking forward to dining in his restaurant. He worked at being gracious, but it was obvious that he felt insulted by Shambless's boorishness. Somehow, we were all crass Americans because of the thoughtlessness of the talk show host.

As we got off the bus, I noticed that Sylvia put

her hand on her companion's arm to restrain him. I heard him say, "Don't be silly, Sylvia. It was a long time ago. Come on. You don't have to talk to him."

She reluctantly followed him into the restaurant.

Rafaela ushered us into a gleaming, dark wood bar. Through the floor-to-ceiling windows, we could admire the magnificent view of the beach and the water. The white damask–covered tables were set with gleaming silver, crystal wine glasses, red and pink roses, and white candles. Most of the tables were reserved for our group of fifty passengers.

Shambless, still loud and obnoxious, sat down at a table for four and waved away other people who tried to sit with him, except for the blonde and the cameraman. "This is my vacation. I talk to people all year long. I don't want to bother with anybody while I'm eating," he said to Señor Delgardo when he tried to bring some of the passengers to his table.

The blonde whispered something in his ear and he smiled into the camera.

"Edit that out," he said to the camera operator, and his voice changed into a mellow, pleasing baritone. "What a pleasure it is to be here in sunny Spain . . . what?"

The blonde said something to him and he continued, even more mellifluously than before. "Or, I should say *rainy* Spain," he said, a slight chuckle in his voice, "because it's the rain here in northern Spain which makes this Green Spain, a lush and beautiful place to see. I want to take you with me on this trip, through picturesque fishing villages, to ninth-century monuments, to the Guggenheim Museum. We'll climb mountains, watch the ocean splash on the shore, visit historic caves." He paused, and smiled into the camera. "I'm so glad you're here with me on this fascinating journey."

He motioned to the cameraman to stop. "That's it for now, Steve," he said in his regular, ordinary bossy voice. "Get some shots of the restaurant and the town around here."

He turned to the blonde. "How was I, honey?"

She took his hand.

"Superb, as always," she said.

He pulled his hand away and tore off a piece of bread from the basket on the table.

Our group was at the table next to his, and we did our best to ignore him.

He looked up as the woman who was trying to avoid him and her companion passed his table.

"Well," he said loudly, "it's been a long time, Sylvia. How's your life going? Still with that soap opera? *Lust in the Afternoon*, isn't it?"

Sylvia stiffened, stopped, and looked at him with such hatred we could feel its heat, then walked past him to a table as far from his as she could find. The man with her glared at the talk show host and followed her to the back of the room.

"I wonder what that's all about," Tina said.

Janice leaned forward and in a low voice said, "I know that guy. His name is Tom Carson. We were in a play together in New York a few years ago." She paused, a dreamy look on her face. "We had a little thing going for a while," she said. "Anyway, I heard that he married the producer of Shambless's talk show, a woman named Sylvia something or other. I don't know what happened exactly, but she left or was fired or something. I heard rumors that Shambless had her fired because she wouldn't sleep with him, and then kept her from being hired as a producer on other talk shows. That's how she ended up producing a soap opera. She hired Tom and I guess that's when they fell in love and got married. I had no idea he was on this trip."

"Hmm," I said. "Shambless makes friends wherever he goes."

We laughed, and looked at Rafaela, who was about to tell us about our dinner choices.

"Since this part of Spain is famous for its incredibly fresh seafood," she said, "the owner of this restaurant has selected the most delicate and delicious dishes." She translated the menu for us.

"Everything is superb here," she said. "You can have cigalas cocidas, which is boiled crayfish with lemon wedges. The crayfish is so fresh it almost sings in your mouth."

"Oh great," Shambless growled. "That's all I need—singing fish. I just want a steak, medium rare, with French fries. And a bottle of red wine, if they have any good wine in Spain. Think you can manage that?"

Señor Delgardo, who was standing nearby, looked at Rafaela. They didn't say anything, but their feelings about this man were unmistakable.

Obviously exerting a great effort to keep his voice pleasant, the owner said, "Señor Shambless, we are noted for our seafood. Try our vieiras al horno, which is—"

"Some kind of horny fish," Shambless said, snickering and looking at his fan at the next table, who giggled.

"As I said before," he said, "all I want is a steak. It's simple. A steak. Medium rare. With French fries. And ketchup."

The guy with the camera leaned over Shambless and whispered something in his ear.

"Oh . . . yeah . . . good point. Wait a sec, Delgardo. Bring me one of your fish dishes with all the trimmings so Steve can film it for the documentary. And then bring me the steak."

Señor Delgardo turned abruptly and went into the kitchen.

Rafaela tried to pretend she hadn't heard all this and continued talking to the rest of us.

"As Señor Delgardo was saying, vieiras al horno is baked scallops. Again, very simple: scallops made with onions, garlic, paprika, sprinkled with bread crumbs, fried, and then put in the oven briefly to brown the crumbs. They are fresh, fresh, fresh."

"Oh blah, blah, blah," said Shambless. "Can you be more boring? I don't care what's on the friggin' menu. Bring the fish. Let Steve get a picture of it. And then bring me my steak, if you can manage such a complicated order."

I'd had enough. "Well, *we* care, Shambless," I said. "So stuff a sock in it until your steak comes."

He turned slowly and looked me up and down and then around the table at the rest of us.

"Ah, the dancing lesbians, I presume," he said loud enough for everyone in the restaurant to hear.

Tina put her hand on my arm, but I'd had enough. I jumped up and confronted him.

"Ah, the impotent talk show host, I presume," I said. I know it wasn't devastating or brilliant, but it was all I could think of at the moment.

"Gini, let it go," Pat said, pulling me back into my seat.

I sat back down, shaking, and looked at Rafaela, who rolled her eyes and told us the rest of our choices.

There was salpicon, a seafood salad, calamari a la plancha, a very spicy squid dish made with lots of hot red-pepper flakes, and bogavante a la gallega, which I ordered after finding out it was lobster and potatoes.

Each of us chose a different main course so we could taste everything on the menu.

When our food came, we were enjoying every mouthful and trying not to hear Shambless, only a few feet away, complaining to the chef, who had come out of the kitchen to find out what was wrong. Shambless complained that his steak was thin and overcooked and inedible.

"It tastes like horsemeat," he said.

This was too much for the chef, a red-faced, portly man, who looked like he would explode. He was about to say something, but the owner quickly led him back to the kitchen and then returned to say to Shambless, "Seafood is the specialty in this part of Spain, señor. Just try these scallops. I think you'll like them."

Shambless glowered at him, shoved the steak aside, and picked up one of the scallops on his fork. He didn't say anything, but finished every one of them down to the last bite, and we were grateful his mouth was full.

As he was pouring his third glass of wine, his devoted fan came over and stood at his elbow. She was a small woman with short graying hair and a lumpy body. She shifted from leg to leg, smoothed her hair, pushed her glasses back on her nose, cleared her throat, and finally tapped him on the shoulder.

He looked up, annoyed at first, but when he

saw that it was his adoring fan, he dredged up a pleasant expression, if not quite a smile.

"Yes, my dear, what can I do for you?"

"I don't mean to bother you, Mr. Shambless," she said, speaking rapidly, "but I just had to tell you how much I enjoy your show. You've taught me so much in the last ten years. I can't wait to tell my friends I met you on this trip. They all think you're wonderful too. We talk about you all the time. So I was wondering, could I trouble you for your autograph? I want them all to know I really met you. "

Shambless paused in midbite and said, his mouth full, "Of course, dear lady. I'm always glad to oblige one of my viewers. Let me sign your menu. What's your name, sweetheart?"

"Dora. Dora Lindquist. Thank you. This means so much to me. I live alone. Your show is my best friend."

The blonde got up and left the table. "I'm going to the—what do they call it?—the señoritas' room? I'll be back when no one is bothering you."

Dora looked up and watched her walk to the restroom. For a minute, her face was serious, but she quickly regained her eager expression when she looked back at Shambless.

He bent over the menu Dora offered him, wrote a message, and then signed it. He took her hand. "It's always a pleasure to meet one of my viewers," he said.

She giggled nervously and held the menu close against her chest.

"What a beautiful ring," he said, still holding her hand. "It's like a locket. How unusual."

"Yes, it has a picture of my little girl in it. She was very beautiful."

"*Was* beautiful?

Dora looked away from him for a minute. I could see that she was trying not to cry. She started to speak and then her voice broke.

"She . . . she . . . died. Last year. She was very sick."

"I'm so sorry to hear that," Shambless said, dropping her hand and slathering a piece of bread with butter. "Could I see her picture?"

Dora backed away and started to return to her table.

"Oh, no. I'm interrupting your dinner. I don't want to bother you."

"It's no bother. I'd like very much to see her picture." He took another swallow of wine.

"No, no, that's all right," Dora said, moving away from him. "I'll show it to you another time. Please, finish your dinner. And thank you."

"It is I who should thank you," he said, pouring himself another glass of wine.

Shambless motioned to the photographer.

"Did you get that, Steve?" he said. "I want a lot of footage of my adoring fans."

"Yeah, I got it," Steve said. "The whole thing."

After Dora went back to her table, Shambless

looked over at us and said, "Hey dancers, you could take a few lessons in femininity from that sweet woman who asked for my autograph. That's how a lady acts. But look who I'm talking to."

I could not stay silent this time either. I was afraid I'd burst a blood vessel if I did. I jumped up from my chair.

"Any one of us is more woman than you can handle, Shambless," I said. "Whatever happened to your three wives, by the way? Didn't they act like ladies?"

Tina tugged at my sleeve and said out the corner of her mouth, "Let him alone, Gini. He's not worth it."

"How can you just sit there and let that idiot say those things, Tina?" I said angrily. "What's the matter with you?"

Pat, sitting next to me, looked up and said quietly, "How many desserts do you think he can eat?"

This made me laugh. I sat down and let my anger go. God bless Pat. I can always count on her to keep me from making a fool of myself. The others all took a deep breath and relaxed.

"Sorry, guys," I muttered. "I'll be good. But that man drives me crazy."

Shambless attacked the rest of his dinner and wine greedily, looking up briefly as the blonde sat down next to him again. She picked at her food and then leaned closer to him and said something that obviously annoyed him.

Mary McHugh

"I told you, we'll talk about that later," he said loud enough for us to hear. "Stop asking me about it. I'll take care of it when the time is right."

"You keep saying that," she said, her voice getting louder. "But the time is never right. I'm sick of waiting. You have to do something about it now."

"I don't have to do anything," he said. "Don't tell me what to do. I told you I'd take care of this and I will. But leave me alone or you'll be on the next plane home."

She took a sip of her wine and ate a few more bites of her dinner. Then she stood up, threw her napkin on the table, and said to him, "I've had enough. I'll wait outside until it's time to go back to the train." She left the table and the dining room.

Shambless ignored her and kept on eating and drinking.

He looked up as Sylvia and Tom passed his table on their way out.

"Had enough to eat, Sylvia? Wouldn't want to get fat. They might kick you out of show business." He laughed nastily.

Tom tried to stop her, but Sylvia came close to the talk show host, leaned over next to him, and in a voice filled with hatred said to him, "I've had more than enough, Dick. Keep your rotten comments to yourself or you'll be very sorry."

288

"What are you going to do, get your own talk show?" Shambless said with a smirk.

"I'm going to do more than talk," Sylvia said, and Tom pulled her away.

"Forget it, Syl," he said. "He's not worth it."

She straightened up and let Tom lead her out of the restaurant.

We sat there stunned, bowled over by Sylvia's emotion.

Rafaela came over to our table.

"You have to have one of our desserts," she said. "They are divine. We have strawberries with whipped cream, almond tart, chocolate tart, and my favorite, tiramisu, even if it is Italian."

We all groaned. "Rafaela, tiramisu is my favorite dessert," Janice said, "but if we eat one more thing, we won't be able to walk, much less dance, tonight."

She laughed. "*Muy bien*," she said. "I won't tempt you. But did you enjoy your dinner?"

We all talked at once trying to tell her how delicious the food was, how beautiful the restaurant was, how much we enjoyed being there.

"Rafaela," Mary Louise said, "I don't mean to be a pest, but is there any chance you could get the recipes for the seafood salad, the calamari, and the lobster? I would love to make them when I get home."

"Let me see what I can do," Rafaela said, and went into the kitchen.

We were interrupted by loud talk from the next table. I heard Shambless say to Eduardo, "I must have a car take me back to the train. I can't ride in that crowded coach again."

"I'm so sorry, señor, but there are no cars available now. I'm afraid you'll have to ride in the coach with the rest of us. It's only a short distance."

Shambless glared at him. "I'm not used to riding on buses," he said contemptuously. "Do something about it. You're in charge here."

Eduardo took the owner aside and spoke to him rapidly in Spanish. The owner nodded.

Eduardo came back to Shambless. "You are in luck. Señor Delgardo, our host, said he would drive you back to the train."

"I hope his driving is better than his food," Shambless said.

He looked up as we passed his table on our way out. "Aren't you girls a little old to be dancing on trains?" he said.

Tina shot me a warning glance, but I couldn't help it. "Aren't you a little fat for a narrow-gauge track?" I said.

My friends dragged me back to the bus before he could answer, but I was still fuming. One woman from the train stopped, smiled at me, and patted my arm as she got back on the bus. "Don't pay any attention to him," she said with a French accent. "He's obnoxious."

"I could kill him," I said. "He's spoiling this whole experience."

As we climbed aboard the bus, we could see Shambless getting into the owner's car. It was a small car and he was a very big man. Steve and the driver pushed and pulled him into the car and closed the door.

When we were all on the bus again, Rafaela came running up and climbed aboard and walked up the aisle to Mary Louise.

"Here are those recipes you asked for," she said, handing her some loose pages. "Enjoy."

"You're an angel, Rafaela," Mary Louise said. "Thank you so much."

Back on the train, we were all feeling way too well fed and not at all sure we could fit into the long, tight-fitting dresses that were slit up the sides so our legs were free to move, stamp, kick, and bend, flamenco style. Covered with silver sequins, they were pure glitter and flash. I loved wearing my gown, because it was the total opposite of my usual costume of a T-shirt and jeans.

"Gini, give me a hand with this zipper, will you?" Tina said. "I think I gained a couple of pounds back there at that restaurant."

"Our dance tonight should use up a few thousand calories," I said.

"*Olé!*" Tina said, clicking her heels and moving

in a tiny circle in our crowded room. "Ready, Gini?"

"*Olé!*" I said, opening the door.

We grabbed our scarves and knocked on the door of our friends' suite.

Our three partners were silver sequined and gorgeous.

"Are we the best or what?" Janice said.

"We're certainly the best fed," Mary Louise said, patting her stomach. "I'm feeling a little stuffed."

"We all are," Tina said. "But we'll be fine once we get on that floor and start moving. Come on, all together now, think flamenco, think clapping hands and flashing feet."

We headed for the ballroom car, waving at the other passengers as we passed through the cars. The ballroom somehow looked smaller than it had in the afternoon.

"Shouldn't we have rehearsed in this car before we actually performed here?" Pat, our worrier, said.

"We'll be OK, Pat," Tina said. "We dance in and out of each other, not in a straight line. We can do it."

Tina clicked on the CD player and the first notes of the flamenco music filled the air.

Just as we were ready to swing out onto the floor, Eduardo ran up to us. He looked frantic, not his usual cool, dignified self.

"Señoras, I have terrible news." He stopped, trying to calm down.

"What's the matter, Eduardo," Tina said, touching his arm. "What has happened?"

He took a deep breath. "He's dead," he said. "He's . . ."

"Who's dead, Eduardo?" I said. "What are you talking about?"

"Señor Shambless," he said. He took a deep breath. "His room attendant, Carlos, found him a half hour ago. He was a mess. Carlos called me and I called one of our passengers who is a doctor—Dr. Parnell. He examined Señor Shambless and said he was dead. But he told me to call the emergency service to take him to the nearest hospital to see if they could revive him."

"Oh, Eduardo, what can we do to help you?" Tina said.

He looked at us pleadingly. "I know it's a terrible thing to ask, señoras, but could you please dance anyway? I don't want the other passengers to know what has happened just yet, and your dancing will keep them here while I figure out what to do."

We looked at each other, straightened up, nodded yes, and told Eduardo not to worry. We would distract the audience or wear out our dancing shoes trying.

MARY LOUISE'S ADAPTATION OF THE RESTAURANT RECIPES

Salpicon de Marisco (Seafood Salad)

1 pound shrimp, cooked, peeled, and deveined
1 pound cooked crabmeat, cut up
¾ pound cooked octopus or squid, cut up
1 small red bell pepper, cut up
1 small green bell pepper, cut up
1 cup small white onions, left whole
1 medium yellow onion sliced
1 cup gherkin pickles, halved
1 cup green olives, stuffed with anchovies and
   left whole

Dressing:

4 teaspoons white vinegar
½ cup olive oil
salt and pepper to taste

1. Mix the seafood together in a large bowl and add the next six ingredients.
2. Whisk white vinegar and olive oil together in small bowl to make dressing. Season with salt and pepper to taste.
3. Pour dressing over salad and toss. Serve at room temperature.

Serves six.

Calamari a la Plancha (Spicy Squid)

1½ pounds raw calamari rings
½ cup olive oil
4 cloves garlic, minced
1½ tablespoons chopped parsley
¼ teaspoon red pepper flakes

sea salt to taste
4 lemon wedges

1. Heat olive oil to sizzling in large skillet. Sauté calamari for about 3 minutes and then add minced garlic (I use 4 cloves, but you can use more if you like really garlicky calamari).
2. Cook until the calamari is golden brown and the garlic smells great but isn't too brown, about 7 minutes. Be careful not to let the calamari get rubbery
3. Add chopped parsley and red pepper flakes. Add some sea salt and garnish with lemon wedges. Serve immediately.

Serves four.

Mary McHugh

Bogavante a la Gallega
(Gallician Lobster with Potatoes)

2 three-pound boiled lobsters
2 medium-size potatoes, boiled and diced
2 teaspoons salt
2 ounces olive oil
½ teaspoon

1. Keep potatoes warm. When lobster is room temperature, detach tails and put one on each plate. Using a sharp knife, take meat out of tails, slice, and put back in tails.
2. Crack open claws with a nutcracker and remove meat with a cocktail fork. Arrange claw meat and potatoes around tails and sprinkle paprika over all. Add salt and olive oil and enjoy.

Serves two.

. . . continued in *Flamenco, Flan, and Fatalities*